ABOUT THE BOOK

When Miss Lavinia Pickerell answers the phone one morning and is told by a strange metallic voice that she owes Square Toe General Store $490.96 for a pair of knitting needles—she knows something is wrong!

Just HOW wrong she and Mr. Gilhuly the postman, and her other friends, Mr. Rugby, owner of the Square Toe County Diner; Mr. Kettelson, who runs the hardware store; Deputy Administrator Blakely, and Mr. Humwhistel, an absent-minded computer expert, begin to learn.

Little by little, Miss Pickerell—with the help of her nephew Euphus and his six brothers and sisters—uncovers the sinister plot of a gigantic computer that wants to take over the world.

Miss Pickerell Meets Mr. H.U.M.

Cataloging
in
Publication
Data
appears
on
last
page.

MISS PICKERELL MEETS
MR. H.U.M.

by Ellen MacGregor and Dora Pantell

Illustrated by Charles Geer

McGRAW-HILL BOOK COMPANY

*New York • St. Louis • San Francisco • Düsseldorf • Johannesburg
Kuala Lumpur • London • Mexico • Montreal • New Delhi • Panama
Rio de Janeiro • Singapore • Sydney • Toronto*

All characters in this book are entirely fictitious.

MISS PICKERELL MEETS MR. H.U.M.

CONTENTS

1. A Strange Call
2. Something Mysterious Is Happening
3. What Next?
4. No More Moonburgers
5. Terrible News
6. The Governor Has a Visitor
7. Miss Pickerell to the Rescue
8. The City of Progress
9. Alone with the Machines
10. Lost in the Maze
11. Miss Pickerell Meets Mr. H.U.M.
12. Through the Vent
13. What Euphus Did
14. Square Toe Farm Is on the Map Again

CHAPTER ONE

A STRANGE CALL

Miss Pickerell was trying to think of a name for her cow when she heard the telephone ring.

"I can't imagine why I've been so neglectful," she said to herself as she walked across her big farmhouse kitchen to the telephone that hung on the wall near the sink. "Every animal should have a name."

Pumpkins, her large black cat, followed her to the telephone, meowing his agreement. He jumped up on the high windowsill next to the sink, pushed down two school books and three sheets of lined paper that were lying there, and rolled himself into a comfortable ball.

"Oh, dear," Miss Pickerell sighed. "Will children never learn to pick up after themselves?" For an instant she regretted ever having asked her seven nieces and nephews to come and visit her. She was glad they were out on a picnic this morning. The house was much more peaceful without them.

The telephone rang again. Miss Pickerell gave up her idea about putting the books and papers away and answered it.

"Hello," she said loudly and clearly into the mouthpiece.

"Miss Pickerell!" a voice began immediately, "This is the Square Toe General Store calling, the Why Not Knit It Department."

Miss Pickerell pushed her glasses more firmly back on her nose, tucked a loose hairpin into place, and frowned. She was certain that she knew every lady who worked in the Why Not Knit It Department. But this voice was unfamiliar. It was high and nasal and not at all pleasant. Miss Pickerell was also nearly certain that no one new had been hired in the Why Not Knit It Department. The manager had been telling everybody that business was terrible.

"Who is this?" she asked cautiously.

A loud click sounded in the telephone receiver.

"I'm afraid we have a poor connection," Miss Pickerell said.

She had hardly finished her sentence when the voice began again:

"Miss Pickerell! This is the Square Toe General Store calling, the Why Not Knit It Department."

Another click sounded in her ear. Miss Pickerell was starting to feel uneasy. It was all very unusual—a voice she did not know, a clicking every few minutes. She did not like it one bit.

"I must insist that you talk a little more . . ." she started to say.

Another click, and the voice interrupted her:

"Did you or did you not pay your bill of $490.96 for one pair of Number 6 knitting needles? Please answer Yes or No."

Miss Pickerell gasped.

"Well, I never!" she replied instantly.

A click came on the wire, but she went right on talking.

"In the first place," she said, "they were a pair of Number 7 knitting needles. And that was exactly fifteen months ago when I was knitting a red cardigan as a birthday present for my oldest niece, Rosemary. They cost sixty-nine cents and I paid for them in *cash*. I must also remind you that you made a mistake like this once before. You should be more careful when you prepare your bills. And . . .”

The click and the voice interrupted again, “Did you or did you not pay your bill of . . .”

Miss Pickerell paid no attention.

“And in the second place,” she said, “I have not bought another pair of knitting needles since. I *did* want to buy a pair of Number 3 needles so that I could knit some good, thick gloves for my middle nephew, Euphus, but I haven’t had a chance to get to the stores. I haven’t even finished a head scarf that I started. I’ve been busy with my planting for the last few months. What with all the rain we’ve been having, I’ve been delayed and—”

The voice was persisting, “Did you or did you not—”

“For your information,” Miss Pickerell said, talking as loudly as she could, “I want to tell you that I don't have the *slightest* intention of paying for something that I did not buy. And that's that!"

Miss Pickerell hung up with a bang. She was almost boiling with anger. She returned to the table and sat down on a straight chair in front of it.

Pumpkins jumped up on her lap.

"Thank goodness that's over," she said to him while she tried to catch her breath. She also reviewed in her mind the ladies who worked in the Why Not Knit It Department. There was Miss Peebles, a kind, stout lady with a decided jaw, Miss Tackintosh who had red cheeks and was always smiling, and Miss Abigail who liked to wear lace collars that set off her bluish-white hair. Miss Pickerell couldn't even imagine any of these ladies talking to her so rudely.

Pumpkins reached up to lick her nose.

"I think I'll make myself some peppermintade," Miss Pickerell said as she hugged him. "That will make me feel better. And then we'll think of a name for the cow."

Choosing a name for a cow was not so easy. Miss Pickerell went over some names in her mind while she brewed a pot of

strong peppermint tea, poured the tea into
a large pitcher filled with ice cubes,
added sugar and a crisp, fresh mint leaf.
She decided immediately against names like
Elsie, Betsy, Daisy, and Clover. They were
just ordinary cow names. She needed a
name that would fit the personality of her
cow, Miss Pickerell reflected, as she sipped
her glass of ice-cold peppermintade and
thought fondly of her cow's especially alert
nature and loving disposition. Miss Pickerell
was a great believer in personality.

She was busy fixing a large plate of
cookies for her seven nieces and nephews

and thinking of their very different per-
sonalities when the telephone rang. Miss
Pickerell froze.

"I'm not going to answer it," she announced to Pumpkins. "I'm simply not
going to listen to those clicks any more."

She returned to thinking about her nieces
and nephews. She concentrated on Euphus
and his incessant scientific experiments. She
wondered what would ever become of such
a strange child.

Then a new thought came into her head.
What if it was somebody else calling? What
if it was somebody calling about Euphus?
That boy could get into trouble anywhere,
even on a Saturday summer picnic.

She raced to the telephone. She nearly
breathed a sigh of relief when she heard the
high nasal voice. But the minute the voice
mentioned $490.96, outrage swept over her
again.

"I've had about as much of this as I can
stand," she shouted. "If the rise in prices
from 69¢ to $490.96 is what my oldest
nephew, Dwight, calls inflation, I'm against
it. On general principles. Even if I didn't
buy a pair of knitting needles lately. And
I demand an explanation!"

Miss Pickerell paused for breath. She glanced at the yellow and orange clock that stood on her refrigerator. Nearly an hour had passed since the telephone first rang. A whole hour that she could have spent in doing something important. Why, she hadn't even visited her cow this morning! The poor animal would be wondering what had happened. Of course, her oldest nephew Dwight had milked her, but still . . .

The voice had stopped, and the click had come and gone. Miss Pickerell opened her mouth to speak. Then she thought better of it. A new idea had just come into her head. She looked hastily at the clock. The small yellow hand had moved exactly one half a minute since the last click. Miss Pickerell checked with her wristwatch to make sure. She looked at the clock again. The yellow hand was moving steadily—one quarter of a minute, on, on, nearly one half a minute . . .

At exactly one half a minute she heard the click. She waited again. She waited a minute this time. There it was! The click and then the voice, "Did you or did you—"

"Why, why," Miss Pickerell spluttered,

her lips trembling, "I . . . I . . . I think I'm talking to a computer. How very, very silly!"

She listened for another two minutes. The pattern was the same: one half a minute for the voice and the click, one minute for her to answer, then the click once more, and the half minute for the voice. . . . There was no mistaking it.

Miss Pickerell quietly put the receiver back on the hook.

"What is this world coming to?" she asked of no one in particular as she sat down again.

Pumpkins meowed inquiringly.

"I can't answer you, Pumpkins," Miss Pickerell said, sighing. "I just don't know. Everything is changing so fast, I'm not even sure from one day to the next . . ."

Pumpkins continued to meow.

Miss Pickerell picked him up to comfort him.

"There, there, Pumpkins," she said soothingly. "There's really nothing to worry about. We don't *know* that anything dreadful is going to happen. And we don't have to fill our heads with such frightening thoughts, either!"

CHAPTER TWO

SOMETHING MYSTERIOUS IS HAPPENING

Miss Pickerell felt much better the minute she began to get ready to go visit her cow.

"About time, too," she said as she put the pitcher of peppermintade on the top shelf of the refrigerator, cleaned up her sink and countertop, and washed and dried her hands. And she felt positively happy when she and Pumpkins walked through the open kitchen door and into the back garden that gave a view of the misty blue hills and of the quiet valley beyond.

"Nothing bad can happen on a day like this," she breathed as she looked out at the country lane winding down between high green hedges to the main road. The rain had made them grow particularly thick this year. Miss Pickerell forced herself to take a look at her neatly arranged but unfinished kitchen garden. So far, the rain had prevented her from planting the cabbages and turnips she had so been looking forward to. But the blue hydrangea bushes that bordered it were in full bloom and the bright yellow roses were climbing all over the wooden gate at the edge of the garden. Mr. Gilhuly, the young, redheaded postman, was waving cheerfully from the mailbox near the gate.

"Good morning, Miss Pickerell," he said, politely lifting his mailman's cap. "Good morning, Pumpkins. How are you both? And how's your cow, Miss Pickerell?"

"The animals are fine, I'm glad to say, Mr. Gilhuly," Miss Pickerell replied. "And I'm fine, too, now that I'm out here."

"I always feel good myself when I get up on Square Toe Mountain," Mr. Gilhuly said.

"It's the fresh, clean air," Miss Pickerell commented.

"Oh, it's more than that," Mr. Gilhuly said. "I don't mean that the air isn't wonderful up here, Miss Pickerell. The best air in the world! But it's more than the air."

"The flowers are beautiful too," Miss Pickerell agreed.

"More than the flowers, Miss Pickerell," Mr. Gilhuly insisted.

Miss Pickerell looked at him curiously. She had never heard Mr. Gilhuly so argumentative before.

"It's your house," he went on. "It's your house with the pointed roof and the checked pink curtains at the kitchen window and the striped pink curtains at the parlor window and, in the front bedroom window, the pink . . ."

"I like pink," Miss Pickerell stated curtly. She was beginning to think there was something wrong with Mr. Gilhuly.

"Oh, I like it too," he hastened to explain. "But I'm talking about something else. I'm not sure that I know how to say it."

"Try," Miss Pickerell said stiffly.

"Well," Mr. Gilhuly said, talking slowly, "Mrs. Pickett's house just up the road has a flat roof, and none of her curtains are the same color, and she has bluebells mostly in her garden."

"I had some bluebells myself last year," Miss Pickerell reflected.

"And Mr. Jamison, on the other side of the mountain," Mr. Gilhuly continued, "has a white house with black curtains."

"Black would certainly not appeal to me," Miss Pickerell said, thinking that she really must be on her way to the upper pasture to see her cow. "But everyone is entitled to his or her own taste."

"That's exactly the point!" Mr. Gilhuly exclaimed. "That's why I like coming up to Square Toe Mountain. Everybody still has a right to be the way he wants to be. It's not the same in some places."

"Pooh!" Miss Pickerell said. "Of course, it is. No sensible person would want it any other way."

Mr. Gilhuly stared at her. He shuffled his feet. He seemed very puzzled.

"I suppose, Miss Pickerell," he said quietly, "that you haven't been down to Square Toe City lately."

"Not for a long time," Miss Pickerell admitted.

"Been busy with your noisy nieces and nephews, I imagine," Mr. Gilhuly went on.

"I am very fond of my nieces and nephews," Miss Pickerell said coldly.

"Well, they're probably not as noisy as they used to be," Mr. Gilhuly apologized. "But that's not what I'm talking about."

"Then what are you talking about, Mr. Gilhuly?" Miss Pickerell asked. She was beginning to think that this conversation would never end.

"Square Toe City, Miss Pickerell!" Mr. Gilhuly burst out. "Square Toe City! You'd never recognize it."

"I'm sure I would," Miss Pickerell replied, trying to make her statement sound final and starting to walk away.

"No, no, Miss Pickerell," Mr. Gilhuly called after her. "You wouldn't know it at all now. Every house is painted dark brown. Every window has a pair of brown cotton curtains. Every garden has only dandelions growing in it."

Miss Pickerell stopped short in her tracks.

"But that's ridiculous, Mr. Gilhuly," she said.

"Maybe it is, maybe it isn't," Mr. Gilhuly said. "All I can say is that when I make my rounds, I'm not sure which house I'm going into and which one I'm coming out of."

Miss Pickerell could hardly believe her ears.

"Will you please tell me why, Mr. Gilhuly?" she inquired.

Mr. Gilhuly took off his hat and scratched his head.

"No one seems to know," he replied slowly. "And the people are even worse. They are very quiet. And they all wear the same things. Last month the ladies all wore gray sweaters down to their knees. And now, they're . . ."

"Someone must know something," Miss Pickerell insisted.

"Something, yes," Mr. Gilhuly agreed. "The orders come from a computer."

Miss Pickerell experienced a sudden sinking sensation in her stomach. She might have known, she thought, that the good feeling she had when she looked out over the mountains wouldn't last.

"A computer?" she whispered. "Orders from a *computer*?"

"Yes," Mr. Gilhuly said. "You're not much of a television watcher, Miss Pickerell, or you would know. Or maybe that channel doesn't reach up into the mountains."

"What channel?" Miss Pickerell asked.

"Why, the one with the computer on it," Mr. Gilhuly stated. "The computer speaks over television twice during the day and three times every evening."

"And the people obey this . . . this computer?" Miss Pickerell exclaimed.

"It's the law," Mr. Gilhuly stated.

Miss Pickerell felt herself trembling.

"It's . . . it's all very mysterious," she said, trying to get a hold on herself.

"You can say that again, Miss Pickerell," Mr. Gilhuly replied. "The only thing I know for sure is that I'm thinking of changing jobs. I can't stand so much monotony. Well, I'd better be off."

He jumped up on his old Rural Free Delivery truck.

"Be seeing you, Miss Pickerell," he said. "Oh, I nearly forgot. I left a circular in your mailbox."

"Nothing else?" Miss Pickerell asked. "No real mail?"

"None," Mr. Gilhuly told her.

"There hasn't been any in a month now," Miss Pickerell commented thoughtfully.

"More like two months," Mr. Gilhuly said. "Funny, isn't it?"

He didn't say it as if he thought it was really funny, though. He and Miss Pickerell looked at each other.

"Do you . . . do you . . ." Miss Pickerell stammered, hesitating even to put the question into words, "Do you suppose that has something to do with the computer, too?"

"I wouldn't be surprised," Mr. Gilhuly said as he closed the door of the truck, tipped his uniform cap again, and put his engine into gear. "'Bye, Miss Pickerell. So long, Pumpkins. Say hello to the cow for me."

Miss Pickerell watched him drive off, clattering first along the winding private lane, then down into the valley, and finally onto the road that would take him straight to Square Toe City.

CHAPTER THREE

WHAT NEXT?

For a long time after Mr. Gilhuly was no longer in sight, Miss Pickerell stood staring into the valley and beyond. She turned around only when Pumpkins began brushing up against her ankles. She picked him up and held him close. The sound of his purring was very reassuring.

"You're right, Pumpkins," she said when she put him down. "There's no use in silly speculations. We'll take the circular out of the mailbox and go visit the cow."

The circular was a yellow piece of paper, folded over twice. She opened it and read:

To whom it may concern:

Every child or animal must be registered and receive a serial number. A current photograph must accompany the name of the child or animal. We repeat: *The photograph must be current.* The photographer will supply the required registration form.

The photographer for this area is Mr. N. C. Squeers. His new shop is located at the intersection of Hickory and Lemon Lanes.

This is an official document.

Miss Pickerell put the circular in her apron pocket and thought about what she had to do. Her seven nieces and nephews were always being photographed by their adoring parents, and she had a fine snapshot that Rosemary had taken of Pumpkins only last week. But she needed a new picture of her cow. She decided to have it taken right away. She was glad that Mr. Squeers was the photographer. He had taken a picture of her cow once. He had done very well. Of course, the cow had been younger then. She was over fourteen now. But she was just as beautiful as she had always been. Miss Pickerell was sure of that.

"And it will be nice to see Mr. Squeers again," she thought as she and Pumpkins proceeded to the pasture. "I'll have a chance to ask him about his son, Covington. I suppose he's still studying to become a veterinarian."

The cow was grazing peacefully in the upper pasture. She mooed when Miss Pickerell approached.

"I know, I know," Miss Pickerell said to her. "I'm very late this morning. But I'll make up for it. I'll take you for a ride in your trailer."

The cow mooed again to show that she understood. She followed Miss Pickerell happily when she led her to the barn where Miss Pickerell kept her automobile and into the red trailer that was attached to the automobile. The cow always rode in the trailer when Miss Pickerell went out for a drive. The trailer had a fringed awning on top to protect the cow from rain or unexpected snow or too much sun.

Pumpkins jumped into the seat beside Miss Pickerell the minute she got behind the wheel. That was his usual place.

It was a short ride to Hickory and Lemon

Lanes. Miss Pickerell knew exactly where it was, right at the turnoff to the main highway.

"I didn't know he had moved," she commented to Pumpkins as she reached the turnoff and looked around for the shop. She found it next to the filling station.

Pumpkins meowed when Miss Pickerell got out of the automobile.

"No, Pumpkins," she told him. "You stay here. I'll be right back."

The sign on the door of the shop said ENTER. Miss Pickerell did so. A tinkling bell signaled her entrance. Mr. Squeers, looking even more confused than the last time she saw him, came out from behind a curtained doorway.

"Oh, good morning, good morning," he said. "Please sit down. I won't be a minute."

Miss Pickerell hoped that was true. Sometimes Mr. Squeers forgot all about the people waiting in his shop for him. Then, when he came out from his darkroom, he was very surprised to see them. But this time he came out before Miss Pickerell even had a chance to do more than notice that some of the pictures on his wall were a little faded.

"How nice to see you, Miss Pickerell," he said. "I suppose you want a new photograph of yourself."

"Not of myself," Miss Pickerell told him. "Of my cow."

"A studio photograph, I suppose," Mr. Squeers replied, nodding.

"I hardly think so," Miss Pickerell told him. "I don't see how my cow would ever get through your door."

"Pity!" Mr. Squeers said. "Studio photographs are always more interesting."

Miss Pickerell said, "Mmmm."

"And I catch expressions much better in studio photographs," Mr. Squeers went on.

"Well, you'll have to do the best you can," Miss Pickerell replied with decision.

"Yes, yes, I will," Mr. Squeers said, following Miss Pickerell outside. "Do you want the picture taken inside or outside of the trailer?"

"I don't think it makes much difference," Miss Pickerell told him. "If you don't like the way the trailer looks in the picture, you can always brush it out."

"Yes, yes, I can," Mr. Squeers admitted. He walked all around the trailer, telling

Miss Pickerell that he had to decide from which angle to take the picture.

"I understand," Miss Pickerell said. "I want a very good picture of my cow. If I like it, I'll have it enlarged and framed later. I'll have to think of the right place to hang it."

Mr. Squeers continued to inspect the cow.

"Would you like the picture full-face or profile?" he asked finally. "Profiles are more interesting. But then you'd have to tell me which profile you prefer. Most customers choose the left one."

"My cow's profile is equally good on both sides," Miss Pickerell said immediately.

Mr. Squeers mumbled his agreement.

"But I think I'd better have it full-face," she went on. "This is an official photograph."

"Ah, yes," Mr. Squeers said. "I'll just go get the rest of my equipment."

Miss Pickerell walked into the shop with him.

"I understand that I get the required registration form that I must fill out from you, Mr. Squeers," she said when they were inside.

"Oh, yes, indeed, Miss Pickerell," the photographer replied. "I'll just look you up in the index file so that I can enter your identification number on the form. I'll do that first. Before I take the picture."

Miss Pickerell wished he would do it after he took the picture. She also wondered why she needed an identification number, but she didn't say anything. She watched him flip card after card in the file drawer that stood on his counter. Every time he was ready to turn the next card, he wet his right forefinger.

"I'm looking in the p's," he said, as he peered at the cards through his reading glasses. "These are all alphabetically arranged."

"Naturally," Miss Pickerell said.

"P . . . Pa . . . Pam . . . Paz . . . Pe . . .

Peg . . . Pes . . . Ah, here we are, Pi . . ."
Mr. Squeers announced.

He turned card after card while Miss
Pickerell watched.

"That's very odd," he said when he
looked up finally. "I can't find any card for
you."

"Not odd at all," Miss Pickerell replied. "I
haven't been here lately."

"Oh, this is not *my* card index file, Miss
Pickerell," Mr. Squeers advised her solemn-
ly. "I didn't make it up. The county people
did. They gave me a card for every person
in Square Toe County. Each and every
one!"

"Well, maybe they made a mistake," Miss Pickerell suggested.

"They *never* make mistakes," Mr. Squeers told her. "They can't. They do it by computer."

Miss Pickerell very nearly groaned.

"And," Mr. Squeers continued sadly, "if you are not listed in my registration file, it can only mean, Miss Pickerell, that you don't really exist."

Miss Pickerell swallowed twice. She stared incredulously. She had always known, of course, that Mr. Squeers was very absentminded. But this was going too far.

"Let me take a look at that file," she said, pulling it out of his hand.

"I'm not sure that it isn't against regulations for you to do that," Mr. Squeers protested.

"Well, as long as you're not sure," Miss Pickerell said, finding her place among the P cards and flipping one card after another rapidly. She looked among the PA's and the PE's too, in case somebody had spelled her name wrong. She even looked under F for FARM and under S for SQUARE TOE. Her card was not there.

"Well, Miss Pickerell," Mr. Squeers stated, "I hate to say that I told you so. But the county has no record of you *or* your farm."

Miss Pickerell refrained from answering.

"And I'm afraid," Mr. Squeers went on, "I'm afraid this means that I can't take a picture of your cow."

Miss Pickerell was really feeling furious now.

"Is that a fact?" she asked sarcastically.

"You see . . ." Mr. Squeers began.

"I don't see at all," Miss Pickerell interrupted.

"Neither you nor . . ." Mr. Squeers tried again.

"I don't see that one thing has anything to do with another," Miss Pickerell said. "What I mean is that I don't see that taking a picture of my cow has anything to do with the state of your index file. But if that's the way you feel about it, I'll say good-bye. Give my best to Covington."

She stalked out of the shop, her head high with outraged dignity. She very nearly let the door bang behind her.

"That man and his records," she said as she got back into her automobile. "He shouldn't even be allowed to keep a file."

She patted Pumpkins while she tried to control her anger.

"Mercy!" she said. "I don't know why I let myself get so worried by such nonsense."

But she *was* worried. Mr. Squeers' files might really not be as disorganized as she thought. And it might really be true that the county people had no card for her. Why, it might even be true that, according to their records, she *didn't* exist!

"That's absolutely the last straw!" she exclaimed. "No intelligent person could ever believe that!"

But her hands shook when she put them on the steering wheel, and she made no move to drive.

"What next?" she asked herself as she remembered all the strange things that had already happened this morning. Her heart thumped wildly.

CHAPTER FOUR

NO MORE MOONBURGERS

The honking of a horn behind her reminded Miss Pickerell that not only did she actually exist but so did her automobile. Another car was trying to pull up near the gas tank at the filling station. The back of her trailer was in the way.

"Sorry, Miss Pickerell," the driver of the car called out. "I didn't want to honk. But I couldn't seem to get your attention."

Miss Pickerell recognized the editor of the *Square Toe Gazette*.

"Oh, dear," she said. "I'm so sorry. I was just leaving."

"And where are you off to on this fine sunny morning, Miss Pickerell?" the editor asked cheerily.

"To the Square Toe County Diner," Miss

Pickerell replied because that was the first place she could think of, and she did not want to tell him that she didn't have a plan in her head.

"Be sure to give Mr. Rugby my best," the editor said.

"I will," Miss Pickerell answered.

She decided, as she drove off, that she might just as well go to the Square Toe County Diner.

"I'm headed in that direction, anyway," she told herself. "And it's about time for lunch. I'll have a moonburger first. And then I'll have one of Mr. Rugby's eclipse specials. It will help take my mind off all this . . . this . . ."

She searched for the right word.

"This silliness," she concluded a little lamely.

Her mouth watered at the very thought of the eclipse special. Mr. Rugby made it with sponge cake and heaping scoops of ice cream.

Miss Pickerell smiled as she remembered the first time she met Mr. Rugby. It was on her visit to the moon. Mr. Rugby was working in the moon cafeteria. Just the thought of him in his big chef's hat with his beaming smile and his double chins bouncing whenever he got excited was funny. And he looked exactly the same these days in the diner where he served free coffee on full-moon nights and put only moon names on the menu.

The Square Toe County Diner was on the outskirts of Square Toe City, right off the main road. Miss Pickerell found a parking space under a nearby tree. She put Pumpkins into the trailer where he and the cow would keep each other company, and she entered the restaurant.

The place was empty. Not even Mr. Rugby was in sight. Miss Pickerell was very surprised. Mr. Rugby's restaurant was usually crowded with happy customers. And Mr. Rugby nearly always ran to the door to welcome new arrivals. When he was very busy, he waved enthusiastically to them.

Miss Pickerell sat down on a high stool in front of the counter.

"Yoo hoo!" she called. "Mr. Rugby!"

She thought she heard someone stirring in the back pantry.

"Yoo hoo," she called again. "Mr. Rugby! Where are you?"

In about a minute she heard what sound-

ed like someone getting up from a chair. Then she heard slow footsteps on a wooden floor. Mr. Rugby came in from the back. Miss Pickerell noticed immediately that his chef's hat had no starch in it, that his double chins sagged, and that he was definitely dragging his feet.

"Why, Mr. Rugby," she exclaimed, "aren't you feeling well?"

"As well as can be expected, I think, Miss Pickerell," he said.

He moved behind the counter.

"Would you like a cup of coffee?" he asked.

Miss Pickerell looked at him carefully.

This was not the jolly Mr. Rugby that she knew. She would certainly ask him a few important questions as soon as she gave him her order.

"No coffee, thank you, Mr. Rugby," she said. "I'd like to begin with one of your wonderful moonburgers, please."

"No more moonburgers, Miss Pickerell," Mr. Rugby replied dully.

"No more moonburgers!" Miss Pickerell gasped. This had never happened in the Square Toe County Diner before.

"No," Mr. Rugby repeated. "No more moonburgers."

"Well," Miss Pickerell said, "then I'll have an eclipse special right away. I've been looking forward to it the whole drive over here."

"No more eclipse specials either," Mr. Rugby replied.

This time Miss Pickerell was really shocked.

"Are you out of everything, Mr. Rugby?" she asked. "I don't see how you can run your business if . . ."

"I'm out of nothing, Miss Pickerell," Mr. Rugby exploded, his chins bouncing up and down very fast. "I have gallons of ice cream in my refrigerator. And more gallons in the freezer. And boxes and boxes of yeast for the sponge cake in my store room. And all the eggs, fresh from the farm. And good, sweet milk and . . . You can come and see for yourself, Miss Pickerell. You can come and see!"

He dashed out from behind the counter and practically dragged Miss Pickerell off with him to the back. He opened and closed doors. He showed her the inside of the huge new refrigerator, of the freezer compartment in the refrigerator, of the tall separate freezer, and of the three dry-food closets. All were full.

"Well, Miss Pickerell?" Mr. Rugby asked. "What do you say now?"

Miss Pickerell had to admit that she was baffled.

"All I can say, Mr. Rugby . . ." she began.

She stopped because she saw Mr. Rugby's recipes. They were scattered every which way on the pantry floor.

"Why . . . why, Mr. Rugby," she spluttered, "your moon recipes! What are they doing on the floor?"

"I was tearing them up," Mr. Rugby said, looking at the recipes mournfully.

"Tearing them up!" Miss Pickerell exclaimed. "Your very own recipes! Why, if they were *my* . . ."

"What's the difference?" Mr. Rugby interrupted, not lifting his eyes.

He took off his chef's hat, crumpled it in one hand, and rubbed his bald head with the other.

"What's the difference?" he asked. "I'll never be able to use them again. I'll never serve moon—"

Miss Pickerell cut him short.

"Mr. Rugby," she said, taking a deep breath and talking very slowly and as calmly as she could, "it is perfectly obvious that you are upset. But I don't happen to know what you are talking about. Now I want you to tell me *why* I can no longer order a moonburger or an eclipse special in your restaurant. And also why you feel compelled to tear up your wonderful moon recipes."

She pushed two hairpins into place and waited.

Mr. Rugby stared at her, his eyes unbelieving.

"You mean you don't know?" he whispered.

Miss Pickerell suddenly felt a cold jolt of fear in the pit of her stomach. She was beginning to suspect what Mr. Rugby would say. She waited grimly.

"It's an order," Mr. Rugby said, still whispering.

"An order?" Miss Pickerell exclaimed.

"Yes," Mr. Rugby said. "I can serve only certain foods. The list comes to me every day. It's always the same, Miss Pickerell. And I am watched, Miss Pickerell, watched all the time."

"Watched?" Miss Pickerell breathed.

"Watched," Mr. Rugby repeated, his voice rising nearly to a scream. "By an eye, an electronic eye in a mirror."

He walked heavily back into the restaurant and over to the far end of the counter. In a corner, on the wall on the left-hand side, hung a large round mirror. Miss Pickerell had seen several of them hanging in the Square Toe City shops. They were supposed to assist the manager of a shop in keeping a sharp lookout on customers in case any of them were tempted to pick something up without paying. The Square Toe General Store had installed three such mirrors on its main floor. Miss Pickerell winced as she remembered her telephone conversation with the computer from the Square Toe General Store this morning. She pushed the thought out of her head.

"I don't see anything electronic about that," she commented to Mr. Rugby. "It's just a . . ."

"You will," Mr. Rugby replied quickly. He disappeared into the back room, came out almost immediately with a ladder.

Miss Pickerell shuddered. She did not like ladders. They made her dizzy.

"I'm not climbing that ladder, Mr. Rugby," she told him, "if that's what you have in mind."

"You will be perfectly safe with me," Mr. Rugby insisted. "I will go first and I will hold your hand."

"I would rather you came behind me," Miss Pickerell said, relenting. "And I will climb three rungs only."

"That will be enough, I think," Mr. Rugby said.

He helped Miss Pickerell up on the first

rung. She climbed the next two with her eyes closed. When she opened them, she saw that she was facing the window that overlooked Mr. Rugby's back vegetable garden, and around the bend she caught a glimpse of her cow's trailer.

"Do you see that tree?" Mr. Rugby asked hoarsely from the rung beneath her. "The poplar tree at the edge of the road? Near your trailer? Some of the wires are attached there."

"Wires!" Miss Pickerell repeated.

"Wires," Mr. Rugby said. "They are connected to wires in back of the mirror. Lift out the mirror, Miss Pickerell, and you will see the electronic eye."

"I will *not* take a finger off the rungs of this ladder," Miss Pickerell declared. "And I have absolutely no intention of lifting any mirror while I'm standing on a ladder."

"Well, it doesn't really matter," Mr. Rugby sighed. "It's there, anyway, watching us."

He and Miss Pickerell retraced their steps downward.

"The wires in the tree, Miss Pickerell," Mr. Rugby said, when they were both off the ladder again, "the wires in the tree

give a signal to a computer and the computer . . ."

He went on with his explanation. But Miss Pickerell was no longer listening. She suddenly felt exhausted and, she had to admit, frightened. She wanted only to get back to her farm and lie down on her horsehair sofa and forget all about this terrible day. Particularly, she wanted to forget about computers.

"I'm going home," she said to Mr. Rugby. "I really must . . ."

"I understand," Mr. Rugby said, puffing a little both from excitement and from his exertions on the ladder. "I have nothing to offer you, no moonburgers, no eclipse specials, not even a crescent waffle, the kind with strawberries that you specially like. All the same, as a friend, I expected you to stay with me during this hour of need. A loyal friend would . . ."

Miss Pickerell was practically bristling with indignation.

"You have no right to say such a thing," she retorted. "I am a *very* loyal friend. But I *have* to go home. I have to . . . to think."

"Maybe you'll think of something," Mr.

Rugby said, brightening up immediately. "I can go with you and wait while you think."

Miss Pickerell sighed as she recalled that Mr. Rugby had always been very optimistic.

"But you can't leave your diner," she answered. "You have your customers to consider."

Mr. Rugby shrugged his shoulders.

"There are no customers, Miss Pickerell," he said. "They don't like the regulation food. Mr. Humwhistel was the only person who came in yesterday. But he's so busy thinking up new inventions, he never knows what he's eating anyway."

Mr. Rugby walked with Miss Pickerell to her automobile.

"I'll drive you, Miss Pickerell," he said with some of his old enthusiasm. "I'll take a shortcut. You know I'm very good at short-cuts."

The last thing Miss Pickerell wanted was for Mr. Rugby to drive her automobile. But she felt too tired to object. She was even too tired to remind him that there was no shortcut to Square Toe Farm. They rode in silence all the way there.

CHAPTER FIVE

TERRIBLE NEWS

Miss Pickerell found her seven nieces and
nephews waiting for her on the farm. She
could see them lined up outside the gate as

soon as Mr. Rugby made the turn into her private lane. Nancy Pickett, who was Rosemary's best friend, was there, too. Nancy had her pet lamb with her. It was the homeless lamb Miss Pickerell had rescued from the skylab a year ago.

The instant the children saw Miss Pickerell they started whispering. Rosemary and Nancy pushed Euphus forward.

"*You* tell her," Miss Pickerell could hear them say to Euphus when Mr. Rugby es-

corted her out of the automobile. "You heard it all."

"You heard it, too," Euphus retorted.

"You heard it first," Rosemary said. "You *have* to tell her."

Miss Pickerell forgot her fears and her horsehair sofa immediately. She checked at once to make sure that no one was hurt. Anything could happen with these children!

"Thank heavens," she murmured when she saw no bumps, bruises, or bandages.

"Aunt Lavinia . . ." Euphus began.

"Euphus," Miss Pickerell told him, "whatever it is that you *have* to tell me is going to wait. My cow needs to be taken to her pasture. She's had a long ride."

"I'll take her," Dwight volunteered quickly. "I'll be glad to go."

"Thank you, Dwight," Miss Pickerell said. "I think it had better be the lower pasture this time of day. It will be cooler for her there."

"Yes, Aunt Lavinia," Dwight said, leading the cow out of her trailer and down into the meadow. The youngest children trooped after him.

"And now," Miss Pickerell said, "we'll

have some ice-cold peppermintade, and you can tell me all about your picnic."

Mr. Rugby, Euphus, Rosemary, and Nancy followed her into the kitchen. Pumpkins stayed outside to play with the lamb.

Miss Pickerell poured peppermintade into glasses for everybody. They all sat around the kitchen table.

"All right, Euphus," Miss Pickerell said. "You were about to tell me . . ."

Euphus looked at Rosemary and Nancy, then down at his glass.

"Yes, Euphus?" Miss Pickerell prompted.

"Dwight should do the telling," Euphus muttered to himself. "*He's* the oldest."

"Age has nothing to do with it," said Rosemary. "Besides, he wasn't even there. He was supervising the twins when . . ."

"I told him later," Euphus insisted.

"Not all of it," Rosemary said. "You—"

"Never mind about Dwight," Miss Pickerell interrupted. "You may as well tell me everything and get it over with."

"Well," Euphus said, still hesitating, "it all began when I wouldn't play those silly old games."

"They were *not* silly," Rosemary protested.

"They were, too," Euphus said. "Especially that potato race."

Privately Miss Pickerell agreed entirely with Euphus. But she remained silent.

"So," Euphus went on, "I decided to listen to my transistor radio, instead. And then Rosemary got out of the race and came and listened. She heard it too."

"Heard *what*?" Miss Pickerell asked.

"A man on the radio," Euphus said, talking very fast now. "He . . . he said that nobody in Square Toe County could own more than one animal. He said that it was a new regulation. He said he was going to start investigating from house to house on Monday. That . . . that's all."

Miss Pickerell felt her heart drop straight into her shoes. She could practically *see* all the lonely animals that had finally found homes for themselves and all the people who loved them so much. She could hardly bear it. . . .

"That . . . that's not possible," she said when she was able to speak again. "You didn't hear it right."

"He did," Rosemary said. "I heard it with him."

"I called my mother," Nancy said. "She heard it too."

"Who . . . who was the man speaking on the radio, Nancy?" Miss Pickerell asked.

"No one knows," Nancy answered. "They didn't say."

Miss Pickerell drew in her breath with a shudder as she stared at Nancy. She noticed that her pretty, brown-flecked eyes were sore from crying. Rosemary and Euphus were trying hard not to cry. Mr. Rugby, on the other hand, was beaming again.

"I'll go call the Governor," he said, racing to the wall telephone.

"I'LL call him," Miss Pickerell said, also racing to the telephone and getting there first. "I'll tell him everything."

She made a list in her mind of the things she was going to report: the voice this morning that kept asking her for $490.96 for a pair of Number 6 knitting needles, the odd things that Mr. Gilhuly told her when they were standing near the letter box that hadn't had any real mail in it for months, the peculiar warning Mr. Squeers had uttered when he could find no record of her in his files, the mirror in Mr. Rugby's diner and the wires that went from it to more wires in a poplar tree. And now this dreadful rule about the animals! *They* must be saved, no matter what. The Governor would understand. He would be able to tell her what was happening. He would know what to . . .

But the Governor's line was busy. Miss Pickerell tried again and again. It was always busy.

She walked to the kitchen door and looked out at Pumpkins and the lamb tossing leaves to each other in the garden. Pumpkins was faster both at batting and catching them. Miss Pickerell felt tears beginning to sting her eyelids. How could anyone even think of . . . ? She turned abruptly away from the door.

She began to pace up and down her kitchen. Back and forth, back and forth, from the green horsehair sofa that stood in the hallway right next to the kitchen to the white enamel broom closet at the other end of the room, and back again. Mr. Rugby and the three children watched. They said nothing.

She stopped in front of the wooden cabinet where she kept her best dishes.

"I must do something," she murmured. "I must do something *fast*."

"What?" Mr. Rugby asked immediately.

Miss Pickerell did not answer. She continued to pace the floor. It helped her to think.

"Rosemary," she said, suddenly, "please pick up those sheets of paper near the window."

Rosemary obeyed instantly.

"Now," Miss Pickerell went on, "give one sheet to Euphus and one to Nancy. Euphus, I want you to make a list of all the people you know in Square Toe County who have more than one animal. And you, Rosemary, make a list of all the people who have no animals. And Nancy, you . . ."

"I understand," Mr. Rugby interrupted, beaming so broadly a gold filling in a back tooth showed. "You're going to spread the animals around, Miss Pickerell. You're going to . . ."

"For the time being, Mr. Rugby," Miss Pickerell told him. "*only* for the time being. I'll think of something else after that."

"Bravo!" Mr. Rugby shouted, clapping his hands. Miss Pickerell wished he would save his applause for when she *did* think of something.

"Nancy," she went on, "you will go to see Dr. Haggerty, the veterinarian, and get a list from him."

"Oh, thank you, Miss Pickerell," Nancy said, rubbing her eyes. "I want to help. I can't bear to think of anything bad happening to the animals."

"I can't bear it myself," Miss Pickerell said, taking off her glasses, absently cleaning them with a corner of her apron, and putting them on again. "But we mustn't think about that now. We have to organize."

"I can help with that," Mr. Rugby volunteered instantly. "I can make out a list of my customers and . . ."

"You and I, Mr. Rugby," Miss Pickerell interrupted, "will pick up the extra animals that need homes and place them in homes where there are no animals. As I said, *temporarily*, of course. People who love their animals do not want to give them up. That . . . that is heartbreaking!"

She walked to the door and looked long and lovingly at Pumpkins and the lamb, and at her cow, grazing contentedly, then turned once more to Mr. Rugby.

"We'll attend to the animal placement today," she said. "Tomorrow, we'll get to the bottom of all this . . . this madness. We'll . . ."

A loud knocking at the door broke in on whatever else Miss Pickerell was going to say. It was Mr. Kettelson, the hardware-store man. He seemed even more haggard and gray than usual.

"Your cow, Miss Pickerell," he panted as he came into the kitchen. "What are you going to do about your cow? They're going to kill her. They're . . ."

"Who . . . who . . . ?" Miss Pickerell gasped, trying desperately to find her voice. "Who is—?"

"The man on the radio," Mr. Kettelson managed to say, while he kept on panting. "He . . . he said that all animals more than eight years old are to be . . ."

He couldn't finish. He sank into a chair.

"You know, Miss Pickerell, how I love your cow," he continued. "She's so gentle, so affectionate, so . . ."

"Stop!" Miss Pickerell whispered. She could not bear to listen. And her head was spinning too. She held on tightly to the edge of the table.

"I'll get you a glass of water," Mr. Rugby said immediately.

"I have the peppermintade," Miss Pickerell told him. "It's right in front of me. On the table."

"Oh!" Mr. Rugby said, looking embarrassed. He tried to help her to sit down.

"Thank you, Mr. Rugby," Miss Pickerell said. "I prefer to stand. I have things to do."

"What?" everybody asked, at once.

"To begin with," Miss Pickerell told them, feeling considerably better now that she had made up her mind, "I'm going to the state capital. I'm talking to the State Senate. *And* to the Governor."

"It's summer now," Euphus announced. "The Senate is not in session."

"Then the Governor will call it into session," Miss Pickerell said. "I'll recommend it to him when I see him."

"You won't be able to see him," Mr. Kettelson commented sadly. "It's a long drive to the state capital. His office will be closed by the time you get there."

"I'm not going to drive," Miss Pickerell told him. "I'm leaving the automobile for Mr. Rugby to use when he picks up the animals."

"I'll go in my truck," Mr. Rugby said, looking cheerful again. "Mr. Kettelson can use your automobile and the trailer. I'll explain it all to him."

"The trains and the buses won't get you there in time either," Mr. Kettelson persisted.

"And there are no more planes going across the mountains," Euphus added. "Not until tomorrow."

"There's helicopter service to the state capital," Miss Pickerell replied.

"No, there isn't," Euphus told her. "The men go off duty at four o'clock."

"It's just after four now," Mr. Rugby said, looking gloomily at the clock.

"Mr. Rugby," Miss Pickerell said, holding herself very erect and fixing her eyes on him steadily. "This is an emergency. There is no time to lose. If the men won't fly me, I'll fly myself. I'll hire a helicopter. They are for hire, aren't they?"

Mr. Rugby opened his mouth, then closed it again.

"I know," Miss Pickerell said, taking off her apron and folding it neatly over the back of her chair, while she tried to ignore the feeling of butterflies in her stomach.

"I've never flown a helicopter by myself before. But it can't be too different from driving an automobile. And to save my cow, I will dare anything. Euphus, please get my umbrella out of the back closet. Rosemary, get me my knitting bag. And make sure that my checkbook and all my credit cards are inside."

CHAPTER SIX

THE GOVERNOR
HAS A VISITOR

As it happened, Miss Pickerell was able to hire a helicopter with a pilot. He chattered so much on the way, Miss Pickerell wasn't so sure she wouldn't have been better off doing the piloting herself.

"Drop me in front of the Governor's office," she told him as they hovered over the state capital building.

"Yes, ma'am," the pilot said. "I'm sure you have important business with the Governor."

"I certainly have," Miss Pickerell snapped. "How much do I owe you?"

She wrote out the check for twenty-five dollars while the pilot was maneuvering the helicopter onto the lawn. The clock in the Capitol dome showed that the time was 4:45

exactly. Miss Pickerell practically leaped out of the helicopter and galloped up the wide marble steps. The Governor's office was the first door on the left. Miss Pickerell went there directly.

A tall, young man wearing a brown and white striped jacket with big brass buttons on the shoulders barred the Governor's door.

"The Governor is occupied," he said before Miss Pickerell even had a chance to open her mouth. "He is studying his map. And he has an appointment at exactly five P.M."

"I'm sure the Governor is a very busy man," Miss Pickerell replied. "But this is urgent. It's really a matter of life and death. There's no time to wait."

"The Governor is occupied," the young man said again. "He is studying his map."

"Please tell him that Miss Pickerell wants to see him. He knows that I wouldn't disturb him unless it was extremely important."

"And he has an appointment at exactly . . ." the young man went on.

Miss Pickerell was beginning to lose patience.

"You sound like a . . . a . . . computer," she said in disgust. "And I insist on seeing the Governor."

She raised her big black umbrella to emphasize the seriousness of her intention. The young man, startled, moved aside. Miss Pickerell seized the opportunity and marched into the oval office.

She spotted the Governor the instant she entered. He was standing with his back to her, facing a huge map that covered the opposite wall of his office. There were colored lights on the map that kept blinking on and off. Just looking at them made Miss Pickerell's head whirl. She kept her eyes partly closed as she walked across the red-carpeted room to where the Governor stood.

"Governor," she said, trying to get his attention.

She had to say it three times, each time a little louder, before he turned around.

"Why, Miss Pickerell," he said, smoothing his moustache and smiling warmly. "How nice to see you! I suppose you've come to take a look at my map. Everybody's heard about it. I've had hundreds of visitors. Why even the President's secretary came once."

"I've come because . . ." Miss Pickerell started to say.

"Naturally, naturally," the Governor replied. "Come and let me show you how it works."

He walked quickly to his desk. Miss Pickerell saw that there was a large console standing on top of the desk.

"Twenty switches. Imagine! This console has twenty switches," the Governor said.

"And thirty-three buttons. I've counted them. And every switch and button activates one or more computer-controlled lights on the map."

He quickly pressed a button to show her. A mass of yellow lights went on. He pressed another. The yellow lights went out and two green ones took their place. He turned a switch and the lights began to bounce.

"With these lights, I can tell at a glance what is going on everywhere in the state," the Governor said, looking very proud. "I'm bringing efficiency and organization to this administration."

"I'm sure you are, Governor," Miss Pickerell said, only half-listening.

"Did you know, Miss Pickerell," the Governor went on, "that the people at Wallow Run had some trouble with their air conditioners yesterday? I knew it in a minute. And when the power at . . . ."

Miss Pickerell stopped listening altogether. She was trying to think of some way she could interrupt that would not be too disrespectful.

"And now look over there," the Governor said, pointing with his chin to the wall behind his desk. There were several gauges on it. Miss Pickerell thought that maybe they had something to do with electrical pressure. She also noticed that a spider was quietly resting on one of the gauges.

The Governor was still talking.

"Yes," he was saying. "It's all here, all the computer connections to and from the map. And let me tell you something else, Miss Pickerell. Not only did I know about the power problem the minute it happened yesterday, but the lights also told me exactly where to go to get more power. I was able to solve the problem in no time, no time at all."

He rubbed his hands together happily.

"Yes," he said with great satisfaction, "that computer has a brain, all right."

Miss Pickerell could no longer contain herself.

"Governor," she burst out, "if that computer of yours is so smart, why hasn't it given me an identification number and why," she added, peering closely at the board of blinking lights, "isn't Square Toe Farm on the map? Tell me that, Governor. Please tell me that."

The instant she said it, Miss Pickerell

could have bitten her tongue. No one talked to a Governor like that. It was . . . why, it was almost against the law. But the Governor didn't seem to have noticed.

"What? What?" he asked. "Square Toe Farm not on the map? We'll look into this immediately, Miss Pickerell. Immediately!"

He walked back to the map, almost bumping into her in his haste. He shook his head when he returned to the desk and began pushing buttons and switches once more. The lights blazed, dimmed, flared, then flickered. The Governor examined them thoughtfully.

"Right you are, Miss Pickerell," he said. "Strange! I can't imagine how Square Toe Farm could possibly have been forgotten. Unless, of course, Square Toe Farm was never fed into the computer. The computer that goes with this map is supposed to have an especially large information storage capacity. The larger the information storage capacity, the more the machine can remember, naturally. I need to check this out."

He put on a pair of round, dark-rimmed glasses that made him look a little like an agitated owl and peered intently through them at all the buttons and all the switches.

"Ah," he said as he pushed a different set and waited. The lights did exactly the same thing they had done before. Miss Pickerell nearly said that she could have told him so.

"Well, well," he went on. "We'll put that right in no time."

He studied a set of directions that was pasted on the side of the console and carefully pushed the keys of a typewriter attached to the console. He threw another switch and blue and orange lights bounced on and off this time.

"All done, Miss Pickerell," he said cheerfully, while he put his glasses back into his breast pocket. "The message has gone out. By tomorrow morning, Square Toe Farm will be back on the map. And now, I really must go. I have to make a speech at the Chamber of Commerce dinner. A very important speech, Miss Pickerell, about computerization in government. It will be printed in all the newspapers."

He took a pair of pearl-gray gloves out of a desk drawer.

"Please, Governor," Miss Pickerell pleaded. "Square Toe Farm is not really what I

came to see you about. It's the animals.
They're . . ."

"Not sick, are they?" the Governor asked.
"No? Well, that's good. That's good."

"They'll be worse than that if we don't do
something," Miss Pickerell said desperately.
"Governor, if you will only please give me a
minute to . . ."

"Oh, come, come, Miss Pickerell," the
Governor said, taking his shiny, black top-
hat and his cane off a wooden clothes tree
that stood in a corner. "It can't be as bad as
all that. I tell you what—why don't you write
me a letter about it? I'll be able to read it
when I have more time. Good-bye, Miss
Pickerell. Do come again, soon."

He courteously extended his hand to Miss
Pickerell. Then, smoothing down his moustache with one hand and jauntily twirling
his cane in the other, he began to stride out
of his office.

Miss Pickerell did not hesitate. She raced
after him.

"Governor!" she called, not caring much
any more whether or not she was talking the
way she should to an officer of the government. "You can't just go away. Time is of
the essence. You have to . . ."

The young man in the brown and white striped jacket raced too. He got between her and the Governor just as she reached the top of the marble steps. The Governor was already running down the steps.

"He has an appointment at exactly five P.M.," the young man said.

Miss Pickerell struggled to get past him. She managed to get her head out from under one of his arms. "Governor!" she shouted. "Governor, you may not realize what is going on. But I do. And I have no intention of letting a computer . . ."

The Governor waved to her.

"Write me a letter," he called over his shoulder. "Don't forget, Miss Pickerell. Write me a letter."

CHAPTER SEVEN

MISS PICKERELL
TO THE RESCUE

Miss Pickerell took the bus back to Square Toe Farm. It was nearly nine o'clock when she got there. Rosemary and Euphus were sitting in the kitchen. Rosemary was holding Pumpkins in her arms. She and Euphus jumped up the minute Miss Pickerell entered.

"What did the Governor say?" they asked at the same time.

"He was very busy with a computer map," Miss Pickerell stated, trying not to sound as furious as she felt. "He told me to write him a letter."

"A letter!" Euphus snorted, walking out of the room.

Miss Pickerell sat down. Rosemary sat down beside her. Pumpkins moved over to

Miss Pickerell's lap. She pulled him up against her chest and buried her head in his fur. She tried hard to think about what to do next.

"Mr. Kettelson placed nineteen animals," Rosemary said. "He just went home. He milked the cow before he left, and he stayed with her in the barn until she fell asleep. He also put your automobile in the barn."

Miss Pickerell nodded without lifting her head.

"Mr. Rugby is still out," Rosemary went on. "He says that he won't stop until he's found a temporary home for every animal who needs one."

"That's good," Miss Pickerell said.

"Lots of other people are helping too," Rosemary said. "Mr. and Mrs. Pickett are helping a lot. And Mr. Gilhuly is out in his mail truck. Dwight is with him. Dr. Haggerty is out in his station wagon and even that lady with the blue hair in the Why Not Knit . . ."

Miss Pickerell looked up. She tried to smile. She knew her niece was doing everything that she knew how to make her feel better.

"Thank you, Rosemary," she said. "Where's Euphus?"

"Here, Aunt Lavinia," Euphus called from the sofa in the hall. "I'm checking up on computers in your encyclopedia."

"You'll find them in the c volume," Miss Pickerell told him.

"I've looked there," Euphus answered. "The information is incomplete."

"I don't see how it can be," Miss Pickerell said, reflecting that Euphus was really beginning to think too much of himself.

"Well, it is," Euphus said. "Your encyclopedia is out of date."

"It's the very latest edition," Miss Pickerell replied. "I bought it from the new door-to-door salesman right after Christmas."

"January, February, March, April, May, June, July," Euphus counted off on his fingers. "It's way out of date."

He came running into the kitchen with a large pad of yellow paper.

"Do you want me to tell you how it all works?" he asked.

He did not wait for an answer. He spread sheets of paper out on the table and began to draw boxes on them with a ball-point pen.

"This one," he said, pointing to the first box, "is the local computer. Every city has one. The city computer is connected to the state computer. That's this box over here. And the state computer is linked up with the federal computer which is connected to the world computer. See?"

"Not at all," Miss Pickerell replied curtly. "I don't see any point at all in that machinery."

"But it's not just machinery," Euphus protested. "My history teacher says the computer is man's best servant."

"And what does your history teacher mean by that outlandish phrase?" Miss Pickerell wanted to know.

"It's very simple," Euphus said. "The computer does what man wants it to do. Man feeds the computer with instructions. Sometimes the instructions are on cards. Sometimes they are on tapes. And sometimes they are electronic signals."

"I know all that," Miss Pickerell said, thinking especially of the buttons the Governor had pushed. "I've seen the machines with the lights and the switches and the buttons."

"Those are only signals telling the computer which instructions to follow," Euphus continued. "Everything is programmed. To program a computer means to provide a computer with instructions. And every computer circuit has a back-up system. That's a substitute system, and it's ready to step in if anything goes wrong."

"And if the computer makes a mistake?" Miss Pickerell asked, coming straight to the point. "If it makes a mistake, what then, Euphus? I ask you, what then?"

"It's corrected," Euphus said calmly. "The main computer is reprogrammed with new data tapes or cards or . . ."

"Or electrical signals," Miss Pickerell finished for him.

"Yes," Euphus said.

Miss Pickerell placed Pumpkins back on the floor and stood up. She felt too restless to sit any longer. There was so much to be done! In so little time! And she was not even sure where to begin.

"What I need to know," she said, half-talking to herself, "is who programs or reprograms this mechanism."

"My history teacher didn't tell us that," Euphus said.

Miss Pickerell began to walk up and down again. She was absolutely convinced now that the responsibility for all the terrible things that had been happening in Square Toe County belonged to the computer. It might not sound very sensible, she knew. But she couldn't help that. Why, Mr. Gilhuly had actually said that the computer went on television. That was where it gave some of its orders. And it was *undoubtedly* the computer that was talking on Euphus' and Mr. Kettelson's radio. On the radio, where nobody could see it! Miss Pickerell thought that it should at least have the courage to show its face. Of course, it was really the person who was programming the computer, a person who hated animals *and* people. She had to, she simply *had* to find him and . . .

"My history teacher didn't tell us who was programming the computer," Euphus repeated apologetically, "but maybe your friend Mr. Humwhistel knows that."

Miss Pickerell stood perfectly still.

"Mr. Humwhistel!" she exclaimed.

"Well," Euphus said defensively, "Mr. Humwhistel *was* in charge of the space-center computers. Remember when you went searching for the weather satellite, he . . ."

Miss Pickerell was already looking up Mr. Humwhistel's number in the directory of personal numbers that hung beside the telephone.

"You can't call him now," Rosemary said. "He's probably in bed."

Miss Pickerell hesitated for only a minute.

"Then he'll just have to get out of bed," she declared, quickly ringing up the number.

Mr. Humwhistel answered on the first ring.

"This is Miss Pickerell," she said immediately. "I want to know the name of the man who runs—excuse me, who programs the main computer."

She paused. Mr. Humwhistel was talking. "Yes," she told him when he stopped. "It is most important. . . . What did you say? . . . It is not a man. . . . It is a master computer brain, known as the Highest Universal Monitor? . . . And it is called HUM for short? . . . No, I don't understand, Mr. Humwhistel. According to Euphus, my middle nephew, someone has to feed requests or instructions to this Mr. HUM so that he can be man's best servant. . . . No, I don't want you to explain it to me in detail. All I want is to stop this Mr. HUM. It is my opinion that he is trying to wipe out the animal life in Square Toe County. As a matter of fact, I believe that he is trying to destroy all life. I spoke to Mr. Gilhuly, the postman, today and to Mr. Rugby and to . . ."

Miss Pickerell paused again. This time, it was a long pause. Rosemary and Euphus looked at her questioningly. She put her fingers on her lips as a signal for them not to interrupt.

"Yes," she said finally. "Thank you, Mr. Humwhistel. I will be there promptly. With the automobile. No, you won't need to hire a car."

She put the receiver down and rejoined the children at the kitchen table.

"He knows what's going on," Miss Pickerell told them. "He's very distressed."

"But what is he going to do about it?" Rosemary asked.

"He is going to let me go with him to the Headquarters of the Universal Monitor tomorrow morning," Miss Pickerell said. "All the computer scientists are meeting there."

"Where is it?" Euphus asked.

"Mr. Humwhistel refused to say," Miss Pickerell replied.

"Maybe he thinks you'd go there and destroy Mr. HUM," Euphus said. "Maybe you ought to do it anyway."

"That would be against the law," Miss Pickerell told him sternly. "But I will take the question up at the meeting. I will tell those computer scientists from all over the world that it has become a matter of life versus the machine."

"Computer scientists from all over the world!" Euphus exclaimed, his eyes shining. "Oh, Aunt Lavinia, may I go with you? May I, please, please?"

"Are you taking Pumpkins?" Rosemary asked. "And the cow?"

"No, Euphus," Miss Pickerell said firmly. "You may not go with me. From Mr. Humwhistel's description, the Headquarters of the Universal Monitor is no place for children. Or for animals, either, Rosemary. You will both take care of Pumpkins and the cow for me. I will be back in the evening. And now it's time for bed."

Miss Pickerell continued to sit at the kitchen table after Rosemary and Euphus had gone upstairs. She thought how fortunate it was that Mr. Humwhistel was her friend and that he was on her side. She thought of her cow who was more than eight years old and had to be rescued and of Pumpkins and of all the other animals who had to be helped. She thought of Mr. Gilhuly and of the dark brown houses in Square Toe City and of the people who lived in them.

"I'll do something about it," she told herself as she put the key under the outside mat for Dwight, and locked the door. "I'll find a way. I *have* to!"

She took a last look around before turning off the ceiling light. Then she walked slowly, with Pumpkins at her heels, to her bedroom.

CHAPTER EIGHT

THE CITY OF PROGRESS

Miss Pickerell was up at dawn the next morning. She dressed as quietly as she could. At the last minute she decided to wear her black straw hat. She secured it firmly to her head with a large hatpin stuck in the middle, made certain that her extra pair of glasses was in her knitting bag, and stopped to take her umbrella. Then she wrote a note to Rosemary. It said:

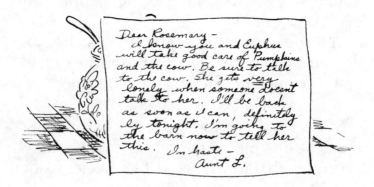

Dear Rosemary —
I know you and Euphus will take good care of Pumpkins and the cow. Be sure to talk to the cow. She gets very lonely when someone doesn't talk to her. I'll be back as soon as I can, definitely by tonight. I'm going to the barn now to tell her this. In haste —
Aunt L.

Miss Pickerell left the note on the kitchen table propped against the sugar bowl where Rosemary would see it when she came in to eat her breakfast. Then she kissed Pumpkins and tiptoed out of the house. It would be nearly impossible for her to get away quickly if the children woke up and started their chattering.

The cow looked up inquiringly when Miss Pickerell unhitched the trailer from the automobile.

"I'm going to meet Mr. Humwhistel at the filling station," Miss Pickerell told her as she patted her on the head. "We have an important errand to do. It won't take more than a few hours."

She looked over her shoulder at the cow as long as she could when she steered the automobile out through the open barn door.

"I'll save her," she whispered. "I will, no matter what I have to do!"

Mr. Humwhistel was already waiting for her at the filling station when Miss Pickerell got there. The weather was very warm but he wore his old-fashioned vest tightly buttoned up to his neck, as usual, and his gold-rimmed spectacles sat on the edge of his nose. Deputy Administrator Horace T. Blakely was also there, standing up very straight and carrying his bulging briefcase.

"Why, Deputy Administrator," Miss Pickerell exclaimed, "I didn't know you were coming with us."

"I am to provide the driving directions," the deputy administrator replied stiffly. "I have three road maps."

"Oh," Miss Pickerell said, wondering why he needed three maps but deciding that it would not be polite to ask. She thought too of how glad she was that his maps were not *computer* controlled. The very word made her shiver all over.

"I am also going in an official capacity," the deputy administrator continued.

"Oh!" Miss Pickerell exclaimed and added courteously, "I was sure of that, Deputy Administrator."

"Please call me Mr. Blakely," the deputy administrator said. "I have asked you that before."

He climbed into the back seat of the automobile. Mr. Humwhistel sat in front with Miss Pickerell. He put his pipe into his mouth immediately and began sucking on it. Miss Pickerell was happy to observe that it was unlit. Mr. Humwhistel could start a fire without even noticing it, he was so lost in reflection most of the time.

"Please start driving, Miss Pickerell," Mr. Blakely advised. "Straight ahead for the time being. We will bypass Square Toe City."

For about an hour they rode in almost complete silence. Except for Mr. Blakely's occasional directions, there was no conversation. Mr. Humwhistel cleared his throat a few times, but he said nothing.

Miss Pickerell was grateful for the quiet. It gave her a chance to marshal her thoughts. She knew exactly what she had to say. No one in his right mind would be unconvinced after she finished her speech. She decided to stop thinking about it. Going over the ideas in her head only made her more nervous. She looked at her watch. It was still very early. She slowed down the automobile from thirty-two to thirty miles an hour and looked around at the country-side.

It was all very unfamiliar to her. On her

right-hand side the mountains had fallen away. A river was flowing there now. Birds stood at its edge. They were chirping and stooping over for sips of water.

"Oh!" Miss Pickerell burst out enthusiastically. "There's a yellow-crowned night heron on that stump over there. Did you see him, Mr. Humwhistel?"

Mr. Humwhistel murmured something under his breath that she could not make out.

"Keep your eyes on the road," Mr. Blakely advised from the rear.

"Yes, Deputy Administrator . . . I mean, Mr. Blakely," Miss Pickerell apologized.

"Continue for one mile," Mr. Blakely said with a sigh. "Then make a left turn."

"I believe it's a right turn," Mr. Humwhistel mumbled.

The deputy administrator consulted all three maps.

"You are correct, Mr. Humwhistel," he said.

Miss Pickerell made a right turn. They were on a narrow country road now. Cows and horses were grazing on both sides. Miss Pickerell noticed a colt trying to run on unsteady legs after his mother, and a cow licking the face of her calf.

"How can anybody want to hurt them?" she asked. "They don't do anything to hurt people."

Mr. Humwhistel grunted sympathetically. Miss Pickerell turned her eyes away from the animals. She couldn't bear to see them so happy and carefree today, when she knew what might happen to them tomorrow. She concentrated on her driving.

The road was going around a bend and widening. Ahead lay a hill. Miss Pickerell pressed her foot on the gas then guided the automobile along a steep downward course. The farmland was giving way to suburbs. The houses were closer together. Shops were starting to appear and main streets with a post office, a courthouse, and a library. Then the small houses began to be replaced by tall apartment buildings and by factories and warehouses. The traffic became thicker.

"We're approaching the City of Progress," Mr. Humwhistel mumbled.

"The *what?*" Miss Pickerell asked.

"Never mind," Mr. Blakely said crisply.

"Drive on, Miss Pickerell, drive on."

"I can't," Miss Pickerell protested. "There's a red light."

But the cars on the road whizzed by her, disregarding the light.

"It must be broken," the deputy administrator replied. "Drive on!"

Miss Pickerell drove on, barely missing a truck cutting across the same intersection.

"Forevermore!" she breathed.

They were approaching another river now. At least, Miss Pickerell thought it was a river because it had a hump-backed, red-bricked bridge over it. Empty barrels, parts of wrecked cars, and a thick, oily substance seemed to be floating on what must once have been clear, clean water. The smell was overpowering. Miss Pickerell could hardly breathe.

It was even worse on the other side of the bridge, where a factory belched smoke and men were throwing factory waste right into the river.

"You can't do that!" Miss Pickerell shouted at them. "You're polluting the . . ."

"We get off this road here," Mr. Blakely interrupted. "Make a sharp left when you reach the two-lane fork."

Miss Pickerell followed his directions. Mr. Humwhistel nearly bumped into the windshield when she made the turn. Mr. Blakely criticized her driving.

"I happen to know a great deal about driving, Deputy Administrator," she replied. "You did not give me enough preparation."

The deputy administrator did not answer. He was busy with his maps. Mr. Humwhistel was squinting through his glasses at the streets they were passing.

"We are almost there, Miss Pickerell," he said. "Drive slowly up to the next corner."

Miss Pickerell did so, her heart in her mouth. The street was very long and, except for two men silently digging dirt out of an excavation site and piling the dirt into a dump truck, absolutely deserted. At the other end of the street two more men, equally solemn, were pouring dirt from another dump truck right back into the excavation site.

"Ridiculous," snorted Miss Pickerell.

"Now," Mr. Humwhistel said, "from this point on, you keep turning. You make a right turn at the end of every second block."

"I see," Miss Pickerell said, although she

wasn't at all sure that either she or Mr. Humwhistel really did. Mr. Humwhistel sounded more as though he might be losing his senses, she thought miserably.

She drove up one back alley, turned into another, and then into still another. All were completely deserted. Every house was boarded up. One was enclosed by a chain-link fence, topped by barbed wire. An ominous quiet hung in the air. Miss Pickerell tried not to shiver. If this was the City of Progress, she thought, she wanted none of it. And she would make it her personal business to see to it that *nothing* like it *ever* happened to Square Toe Mountain. She . . .

"Stop!" Mr. Blakely said, startling her.

Miss Pickerell jammed down the brake pedal. The automobile shook to a halt. Mr. Humwhistel helped Miss Pickerell out. Mr. Blakely joined them on the street.

They were standing in front of a building that looked like a cement fortress. The walls were thick and gray and didn't curve anywhere. There were only two small windows. They were black with dirt and had heavy bars on them. A murky disused canal on one side of the building made it look still more sinister.

"This way," Mr. Blakely stated.

"Where?" Miss Pickerell asked. "I don't see any door."

"The door will slide open to admit us," Mr. Humwhistel told her.

"It will also shut behind us when we have entered," Mr. Blakely said.

Miss Pickerell closed her eyes. She began to rehearse her speech.

"I will definitely say," she told herself, "that if we don't watch out, the computer will take over and proceed to wipe us *all* out. I will then . . ."

She gasped as Mr. Humwhistel gently pushed her through the door that silently slid open and just as silently slid shut behind them.

CHAPTER NINE

ALONE WITH THE MACHINES

She did not open her eyes until she heard the sound of a harsh, grating voice. Its jarring tones echoed in every corner of the room. It gave Miss Pickerell goose bumps. She rubbed her arms up and down to warm them while she looked around. The room, long and so narrow that it seemed almost like a corridor, was lit only by a naked electric bulb. The bulb dangled at the end of a steel chain suspended from the ceiling. As the chain swung back and forth, it lit up parts of the room and cast shadows in others. Machines were everywhere. They stood like menacing sentinels against every inch of wall space. Miss Pickerell rubbed her arms harder and wished she had thought to bring a sweater along. She also wished she

could see where the voice was coming from.

"Follow me," the voice repeated. "I am your guide."

She saw the shadowy outline then, a massive figure in green-checked overalls, wedged between two machines at the far end of the room.

"Mercy!" she breathed.

Mr. Humwhistel and the deputy administrator hurried forward. Miss Pickerell tried to keep up with their long strides. She paused once to catch her breath. She edged away almost immediately. A machine at her side, shrouded in a black curtain, was talking. Miss Pickerell thought it sounded like the cackling of a disgruntled hen.

"How silly!" she said, as she quickly moved on.

"Not at all," Mr. Blakely, who had slowed his pace to accompany her, replied.

"Oh?" Miss Pickerell exclaimed, pausing again. "What do you . . . . ?"

The deputy administrator did not stop to explain. He put his hand under Miss Pickerell's elbow and firmly hurried her along until they caught up with Mr. Humwhistel and the guide at the far wall.

ARR-R-GH

"I'm sorry," Miss Pickerell said at once. "I didn't mean to keep you waiting."

Mr. Humwhistel smiled weakly. The guide said nothing. He stood impassively before her. He had a huge, round head, a fierce, brown moustache, and a very sallow complexion.

"I'm very sorry," Miss Pickerell repeated, shivering a little.

The guide stared with unblinking eyes. Miss Pickerell tried to meet his gaze. She thought indignantly that he might at least

have the courtesy to accept her apology. After all, she had not *deliberately* kept him waiting.

Still staring, he put his right hand up on the wall. A door slid open in response to his touch. They walked into another room. It looked exactly like the one they had just come out of. Mr. Humwhistel and Deputy Administrator Blakely alternately offered Miss Pickerell an arm to lean on while they were walking through the second room. Miss Pickerell thanked them but refused.

By taking very deep breaths and jogging, she was able to keep up. They were all together when the guide stopped at the far end of the second room.

"Follow me," he said.

Miss Pickerell nodded. She wondered though why he had to say it every time they stopped. It wasn't as if they could do anything *but* go with him.

"Follow me," he said again. And then he repeated it.

Miss Pickerell looked at him curiously. She noticed that his lips did not move when he talked. His mouth opened and closed but his lips definitely did not move. She thought suddenly of a doll she had once bought for Rosemary. It was a doll with an old-fashioned china face and a key built into the back of its canvas body. When you turned the key, the doll opened its mouth and said, "Mama" three and a half times. Then you had to wind it up again. Miss Pickerell laughed out loud.

"Why, he . . . he's nothing but a wind-up toy," she stammered. "Only, it's electricity that makes him talk instead of a coil of wire attached to a little key. His machinery must have gotten stuck just now. It must have—"

"Shhh!" the deputy administrator hissed.

"I don't care," Miss Pickerell insisted. "In my opinion, he's nothing but a robot. And I think it's perfectly idiotic to be afraid of a—"

Mr. Humwhistel gave her a sharp warning look.

Miss Pickerell stopped talking. But she still thought that he and the deputy administrator were being foolish. Personally, she did not intend to feel troubled by the guide any more.

They walked through another room. And another. And still another. Every room was the same. Machines, machines, machines . . . Some were silent and menacing. Some were whispering or roaring behind dark curtains. And everywhere naked electric bulbs swung back and forth, back and forth. They made Miss Pickerell's head reel. She was just beginning to think that she might have to accept the offer of a strong arm to lean on when they entered a room with some chairs in it. Miss Pickerell sank into the nearest one.

"This must be the conference place," she

decided as she looked around. The room contained a long wooden table, several straight-backed chairs, and two especially large machines that stood on either side of a mantelpiece. She called out to ask Mr. Humwhistel why no one was here yet. He was busy talking to Deputy Administrator Blakely at the other end of the room. The deputy administrator and the guide were listening intently.

"Well, I'll just wait until they finish," she told herself.

She hadn't realized how tired she was until she actually sat down. Her head was really spinning and her stomach felt empty. She remembered that she had eaten no breakfast this morning and no dinner or even lunch yesterday. As a matter of fact, she had had nothing but two glasses of peppermintade since breakfast yesterday. She smiled as she thought of the delicious taste of the cold peppermintade.

"I'll be fine," she told herself comfortingly. "I'll just rest a while. And maybe there will be some coffee when the conference starts."

She looked up to see Mr. Humwhistel waving at her.

"That's all right," she said when he turned back to talk to Deputy Administrator Blakely. "I don't mind waiting."

She glanced around the room again. It had a window in it, she noticed, one of those with the bars that she had seen from the outside. But like the dead white walls and the mantelpiece, it was completely bare.

"Now, if this were my conference room," she reflected, "I'd know what to do with it. First, of course, I'd wash the window. With good, strong soap. Then I'd hang some drapes up to hide those ugly bars. Some fresh flowers would be nice too. And some pictures on the walls . . . Or maybe some wallpaper . . . A small rosebud pattern might be suitable here. And I think I'd put a nice big clock on that mantelpiece. I'd certainly bring in a closet. Where are the conference people supposed to put their hats and coats when there is no closet?"

She was sure that Deputy Administrator Blakely would agree with her. His own office was so neat and tidy. Mr. Humwhistel never even noticed what a room looked like. She glanced up to see whether they had finished talking.

"Oh, no!" she gasped as she saw them

walking quickly toward the door. She realized suddenly that Mr. Humwhistel had not been waving to say that he would be right over. He had been gesturing for her to join them.

"Oh, no!" she screamed. But they did not hear her. They were walking out of the room. And the door slid shut behind them.

She raced to the wall, shouting, "Mr. Humwhistel! Mr. Blakely!" She rapped on the wall with her umbrella. Nobody heard her. Nobody could possibly hear her over the noise the two machines had started to make. They rumbled, they roared, they hissed, they sputtered, they roared again.

Miss Pickerell put her fingers into her ears.

"Stop it!" she shouted at the machines. "Stop it, please!"

The machines did not stop. They started to move, first from side to side, then from front to back. They seemed to be rolling toward her.

"No, no!" she screamed, while the panic rose in her.

She backed up against the wall as far from the machines as she could get. The machines roared and moved closer.

"This can't be happening," she whispered as she gritted her teeth and told herself that she must be reasonable. "Computers don't attack people. They *can't*! I must be dreaming. I must be imagining."

But she wasn't completely sure that it was her imagination when she remembered what Euphus had told her about how the computers were linked up to each other and when she thought of what Mr. Humwhistel had said about Mr. HUM, the Highest Universal Monitor. Maybe Mr. HUM was telling the two computers to attack her. Maybe they were only carrying out his instructions. Maybe . . .

She couldn't think any more. Her head was going round and round. Her legs felt like water. She crouched against the wall and glared at the machines steadily advancing and shaking the floor as they came. They shook it so hard that she felt the vibrations going up through the soles of her feet, up her legs, right up to her eyes, and out the top of her head until she could no longer see straight. Then suddenly, it seemed, the machines started to go backward. She felt herself toppling over. She was slowly but surely blacking out.

CHAPTER TEN

LOST IN THE MAZE

Miss Pickerell struggled to regain consciousness. She forced her eyes open and made her tottering legs stand up. She was very dizzy and couldn't focus too well. But she was able to see that the machines were back in their original positions beside the mantelpiece. They were also completely silent.

"Forevermore!" Miss Pickerell whispered. "I was sure they were moving. That's what comes of not eating for so long. An empty stomach can give you a nightmare at any time."

But she wasn't so sure that the machines had not been moving when she examined them more closely. The one on the right-hand side seemed to be standing at a slightly different angle. And the machine on the left was jutting out a little, instead of standing exactly parallel with the mantelpiece.

"Almost as if it didn't have quite enough time to get back," Miss Pickerell speculated and thought again about the idea of messages from Mr. HUM. She remembered that men in outer space acted on signals from people in a center on earth. She supposed such a system could be worked out between computers too. A little cold shiver ran through her as she considered that computers were getting to behave more and more like humans. And she shuddered when she recalled that she had not seen a single living creature since she, Mr. Humwhistel, and the deputy administrator had entered the Headquarters of the Universal Monitor.

"Not even a plant!" she murmured and then told herself that she *had* to stop thinking about these things. But she couldn't help taking another quick glance at the computers.

"Why," she gasped, "they look like human *skeletons!*"

She stared with horror at the tapes on the front of each computer. They seemed to stare back out of hollow, unseeing eyes.

And the rows of buttons farther down made her think of teeth in a hideously grinning mouth. She could almost hear her own terrified breathing as she turned away and gave her attention to ways of getting out of the room. The first thing she had to do was to find the door. She surveyed the wall.

"Well," she said, sliding her hand up and down, "if a robot can touch a wall and make it open, I can too. There must be a hidden panel somewhere."

She tried to figure out exactly where the guide had touched the last wall. It was in a place that was approximately level with his chest. That would be about five inches above her head, she estimated. She put her umbrella and her knitting bag down on the floor. She carefully passed her hands along the area that she considered right. Nothing happened.

"Maybe the panel is in a different place on every wall," she said. "Maybe there are even two panels. I'll start from the beginning and try everywhere."

She got down on her hands and knees. Inch by inch, she fingered the bottom part of the wall. Then she moved a little higher, then still higher. It was when she was getting up from her knees and weakly leaning against the wall for support that a door suddenly slid open.

"Forevermore!" she breathed, hastily grabbing her bag and her umbrella and rushing through the opening before the door closed behind her.

"My," she panted when she was on the other side. "I might never have found that panel again."

She hastily examined her new surroundings. She had entered what seemed to be a tunnel. She raced ahead. The tunnel was dark and she could barely see where she was going. She nearly fell when the floor began to slope upward.

"I must be going over a ramp," she said. She remembered how she and Mr. Rugby had climbed up and down ramps on the moon. She had been annoyed with Mr. Rugby because he had told her he knew a shortcut and the way over the ramp had been anything but short. But he had been somebody to talk to. And with the lack of gravity on the moon, they had practically floated along. Here she was alone and frightened and her feet hurt and she was beginning to get a splitting headache.

She drew a deep breath and tried not to think about the waves of fatigue that seemed to be sweeping over her. She was walking downhill now. And a light was coming from the end of the tunnel.

"Mercy!" she exclaimed as she stepped into a room absolutely ablaze with electric bulbs. They swung from practically every inch of the ceiling and shone on white tiled walls and on computers of every shape and size that filled the room. The lights on the computers were also flashing. Miss Pickerell felt herself becoming dizzy again. She tried to shade her eyes with her hands. It didn't help much.

"I'll just open my umbrella," she decided, feeling thankful she had brought it with her.

The umbrella shielded her from the unblinking glare of the ceiling lights. By keeping her eyes half-closed, she was able to make her way past the computers to the other end of the room.

"Oh," she said, as she unexpectedly saw a door with an ordinary knob on it. She turned the knob quickly and walked into a very ordinary-looking hallway. She nearly laughed out loud with relief.

"The conference room must be at the end of the hall," she reassured herself, as she closed her umbrella. "That's where conference rooms usually are."

When she reached the door, she stopped to straighten her hat and began to rehearse her speech again.

"I may even tell them about those computers moving," she thought as she knocked and, without waiting for an answer, walked in. "Forevermore!" she whispered, finding herself in the same tunnel. "What do I do now?"

She leaned on her umbrella and tried to steady her nerves.

"I mustn't panic," she told herself. "I mustn't panic. I have to think."

But she was so tired, all she could think of was sitting down somewhere, with her feet tucked under her. . . .

"Like Pumpkins," she murmured.

The thought of Pumpkins made her stand up straight immediately.

"I probably missed a door on the way,"

she told herself resolutely. "I'll start over. And I'll go more slowly this time."

She walked through the dark tunnel, up and down the ramps, peering as hard as she could to the right and to the left and then into the room with all the fierce lights and through it slowly, carefully, into the hall-way, and up to the tunnel again.

"I'm lost," she said helplessly. "Lost in this terrible maze."

She stood quite still, clutching her knitting bag and her umbrella with shaking hands. She wondered if Mr. Humwhistel and the deputy administrator had missed her and if they were trying to find her. They might be too busy at the conference with all those important scientists even to think about her. She would have no chance to tell the scientists about what the computer was doing to the animals and the people in Square Toe County. Maybe Mr. Humwhistel would say it for her. Maybe he would save her cow and all the other animals who were in danger. . . .

Suddenly, a new, agonizing thought came into her head. Maybe Mr. Humwhistel and the deputy administrator were being prevented from looking for her. That would explain why they hadn't come searching. She wondered if she would ever see her beloved cow again or her delightful Pumpkins or her seven nieces and nephews whom she was really very fond of, or even her farm, her lovely, quiet, orderly Square Toe Farm.

"No! No!" she burst out, banging on the floor with her umbrella. "I can't let this happen. I *won't*. I'll call for help. I'll *scream* for help!"

She took a deep breath to make her voice as loud as possible and opened her mouth. A yanking from the other side of the door leading back from the tunnel froze the scream on her lips. Two robots, even grimmer and more massive than the robot guide, loomed before her. They lunged simultaneously forward. They picked her up by the arms and, dangling her between them, walked down a corridor she had never seen before and through a wall that quickly opened on signal and, just as quickly, closed again. A deafening, clanging alarm sounded all around her.

CHAPTER ELEVEN

MISS PICKERELL
MEETS MR. H.U.M.

The clanging stopped finally. The robots
put her down. Miss Pickerell was so furious,
she forgot all about being frightened.

"How dare you!" she fumed, turning to
the robot on her right. "How dare you
behave this way!"

The robot seemed to hang his head. But
the robot on her left only glared, both at her
and at the other robot. The one at the right
responded to the glare by squeezing her
arm. He let go when the second robot
glared again. Miss Pickerell was thinking
that the second one was probably a newer
model or an inexperienced substitute when
she noticed the computer in front of her. It
was larger than any machine she had ever
seen in her life. A huge screen, with more

wires than she could count attached to it, hung just above the computer. On the right, a giant conveyor belt stretched out. Next to it, a number of huge, pneumatic mailing tubes stood upright. They were just like the tubes the Square Toe General Store used for getting change back from the office upstairs to waiting cash customers. Only these tubes were at least a thousand times bigger.

A voice coming from the computer brought her back to attention. The computer was talking to her.

"I am Mr. HUM," it said, in a deep, monotonous voice. "Chief Security Computer for the planet Earth."

Miss Pickerell gasped weakly.

"How do you do, Mr. HUM," she said as politely as she could and added quickly, "I'm very glad to meet you, finally. I have a number of questions to take up with you."

"Please give me your computer identity number," Mr. H.U.M. replied.

Miss Pickerell had no idea as to what he was talking about. She had never heard of a computer identity number, unless it was what Mr. Squeers, the photographer, had hinted at when he was looking her up in his strange files. In that case . . .

"You heard the order," the robot on the left muttered angrily, taking hold of her arm.

"You heard what Mr. H.U.M. asked for," the robot on the right said, taking hold of her other arm.

Both of them proceeded to tighten their grip.

"Ouch!" Miss Pickerell winced. "Stop that!"

The robots relaxed their hold.

"I must insist that you refrain from talking to me in this manner," Miss Pickerell told them acidly, while she squirmed out of their grasp. "Why, my seven nieces and nephews have better manners than you. And they're just children. What you need, my good men . . . my good robots, I mean, is a course in common courtesy."

She turned to Mr. H.U.M.

"Personally, Mr. HUM," she told him, "I wouldn't think for an instant of having men or whatever they are who behave like . . . like gangsters work for me. They can only give you a bad reputation."

"Please give me your computer identity number," Mr. H.U.M. repeated. "Please give me your computer identity number. Please give . . ."

Miss Pickerell wondered for a minute whether his connections had gotten stuck too, like the robot guide's.

"Mr. HUM," she interrupted, "I would gladly give you my computer identity number if I had one. As it happens, I had never heard of a computer identity number until I took my cow to have her picture taken. And if it hadn't been for the fact that Mr. Gilhuly, the postman, left a circular in my mailbox, I wouldn't have known about the regulation for taking pictures of animals. But I can certainly give you all the information you want, Mr. HUM. I'm Miss Lavinia Pickerell from Square Toe Farm. I came here to . . ."

The computer suddenly stopped talking. Green lights flashed along its top. Orange lights on the bottom blinked back. Tapes inserted between the green and orange lights began to whirl. A voice from a smaller computer that Miss Pickerell had not even noticed said, "Civilian Information Bank operative. Civilian Information Bank ready for questions."

Mr. H.U.M. spoke again. Miss Pickerell couldn't make out what he was saying. The tapes were whirling so loudly she couldn't hear anything else. She tried to put her hands over her ears to shut out the noise. The robots pushed them down. Then the metallic voice from the second computer said very distinctly, "We have no record of a Miss Lavinia Pickerell from Square Toe Farm. We have no record of Square Toe Farm. We have no data in cross-index file."

"I can explain all that, Mr. HUM," Miss Pickerell said promptly. "I mentioned it to the Governor only yesterday. He promised me that he would . . ."

"Spy!" Mr. H.U.M. crackled.

Miss Pickerell cringed.

"But . . . but that's ridiculous," she stammered. "Anyone in Square Toe County will tell you that I . . ."

"Spy!" the two robots roared. They grabbed her arms and squeezed. The pain was agonizing. Miss Pickerell thought she was surely going to faint again. She tried hard to find her voice so that she could say something. When she was able to speak, it was in a high squeak that she hardly recognized.

"There *must* be a record of me . . . somewhere," she said because it was the only thing she could think of and because it was a short sentence and easy to get out.

"We'll check," Mr. H.U.M. said. "We'll make a planet check. We'll learn where you belong. Spy!"

"Spy!" the robots repeated.

The tapes whirled again. The lights flashed off and on, off and on. Whistles and wheezes seemed to come from all over the room. Then a third voice barked, "Affirmative! Affirmative! Miss Lavinia Pickerell is registered on the planet Mars."

"Oh, no!" Miss Pickerell screamed so vigorously that she felt herself turning purple in the face. "I was up on Mars only once. I went there by accident. I didn't know what the space ship was doing in my pasture and I . . ."

The whistling started again. The same voice spoke.

"Check and double check proceeding," it said.

The two robots looked up. Miss Pickerell

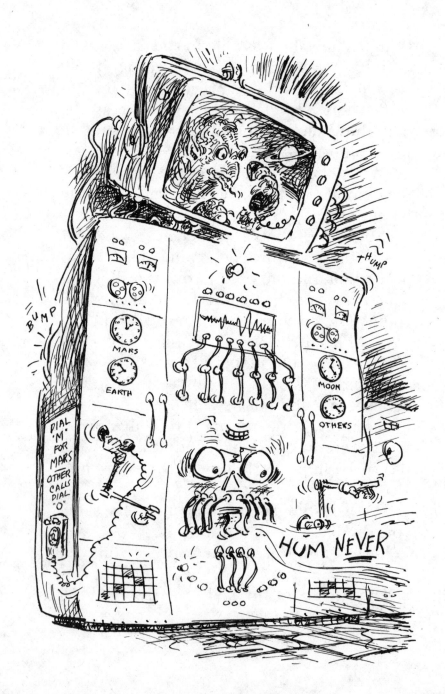

followed their eyes. They were staring at the screen above Mr. H.U.M. She watched in horror as a huge figure that looked like a prehistoric monster appeared on the screen.

"Mars?" Mr. H.U.M. asked.

"Mars!" the creature replied. "Mars on interplanetary communication!"

"Oh, no," Miss Pickerell gulped. "He couldn't be from Mars. There is no life on Mars."

"*You* didn't see any life on Mars," Mr. H.U.M. said. He pointed to the screen.

MAKES A MISTAKE!

"Proceed with your information, man from Mars," Mr. H.U.M. directed.

"We have both a record and a picture of Miss Lavinia Pickerell," the monster said. "She belongs to us."

The image on the screen changed. A picture of Miss Pickerell appeared.

She began to laugh wildly. She had an idea that she might become hysterical at any moment.

"That's the picture from the *Square Toe Gazette*," she shouted. "They took it when I came back to Earth. My cow was in that picture too. She was standing right next to me. Somebody tried to cut her out of the picture but she's still there. Why, you can see one of her horns right under my hands. I was patting her head. You should call the editor of the *Square Toe Gazette*, Mr. HUM. He'll verify every word I'm saying."

She paused for breath.

"You're making a mistake, Mr. HUM," she concluded. "A terrible, terrible mistake!"

Silence followed her pronouncement.

"Miss Pickerell . . ." Mr. H.U.M. began.

There was a faint hesitation in his voice.

For one wonderful moment Miss Pickerell thought he might be starting to become reasonable. It was a false hope.

"HUM never makes a mistake!" he continued hollowly. "Prepare to launch subject back to Mars. Immediately!"

The two robots took hold of her arms, picked her up, and marched to the right of Mr. H.U.M.

"Stop that!" Miss Pickerell shouted indignantly. "Take your hands off me and call the editor. Call him this minute!"

The robots paid no attention. One of them held her while the other unsealed a giant, clear, plastic pneumatic tube. Together they put her into it. They resealed the tube. The last thing Miss Pickerell heard was Mr. H.U.M. saying, "Push the button that will launch her via the conveyor belt onto the rocket for Mars!"

CHAPTER TWELVE

THROUGH THE VENT

The tube whooshed upward. Miss Pickerell, flat on her back inside, screamed for help. None came. And she rode in the tube as it zoomed up, then down, then up again, then turned sharply right, then left, and up, up, up. When she saw lights shining down on her from the outside of the tube, she was sure that she was near the stars and would soon be entering outer space. She couldn't even continue to cry for help. Her throat felt paralyzed. Her breathing came in short gasps. Just when she thought she could stand it no longer, the tube shot down, down, down until it landed with a bang that hurled her up against the roof of the tube with such a thud that she screamed without even trying.

She suddenly heard shouts all around

her. Someone who kept asking, "What is it? What is it?" unsealed the tube. Miss Pickerell, too exhausted to move, just stared. She seemed to be in an enormous cage. Tall, thin wires stood at her head, her feet, her sides. But at the top of the wires, she saw people with kind, worried faces. Human faces! One of them, a plump, blonde young woman held Miss Pickerell's hands while two men put their arms under her shoulders and helped her to stand up. And then she saw Mr. Humwhistel who, between sucks on his pipe, was muttering, "Where were you? Where were you? We searched everywhere!" Mr. Blakely, standing near him, was scrutinizing her from head to toe and earnestly inquiring, "Are you hurt, Miss Pickerell?"

She could not answer. It was all she could do to walk, with Mr. Humwhistel's and Mr. Blakely's support, to a seat at a large oval table, covered, she noticed, by a shining sheet of glass. The men gathered around her. The plump young woman told them to stand back and give her air and asked her if she was feeling better.

Miss Pickerell nodded.

"Mr. HUM told the robots to launch me up to Mars," she said, sure that she was not making herself clear but not feeling up to going into any long explanation.

"Mr. HUM!"

"Mr. HUM!"

"Mr. HUM!"

Everyone in the room repeated the name in a shocked whisper. The young woman was the first to pull herself together.

"Well, they pushed the wrong button," she said. "You went through the vent instead, the vent that leads to the conference room and right into our incoming mail basket."

"And when I thought I was up in the stars," Miss Pickerell remarked, "I was probably just seeing the lights in the ceiling of the tube duct."

The young woman nodded, introduced herself as Ms. Agatha Whitechurch, the chairlady of the conference, and said she'd better get the scientists to go on with the meeting. She walked to the head of the table and rapped on it with a pencil. Miss Pickerell noticed that the big wire basket was standing right there. She also observed gratefully that Ms. Whitechurch, though obviously upset, was quite capable and very conscientious about her job as chairlady.

"The meeting will come to order," she announced in a grave voice. "We have urgent matters to discuss."

The scientists sat down at once. Mr. Humwhistel and the deputy administrator sat on either side of Miss Pickerell. A handsome, middle-aged man, wearing tight black pants and a white turtleneck sweater smiled encouragingly to her from a seat directly opposite. An older man, small and very thin, leaned across the table and said he could imagine what she'd been through. He then raised his hand for the chairlady's attention.

"Ms. Chairlady," he said, when she recognized his wish to speak, "I want to go on record as stating that I think the computers have gone mad."

"Hear! Hear!" everybody shouted. Nearly everybody raised his hand to ask for a chance to talk.

Ms. Whitechurch recognized an extremely tall man, sitting next to Mr. Humwhistel.

"As we all know, Ms. Chairlady," he said when he stood up, "the statement by the previous speaker is utterly impossible. Computers are man-made machines. Even Mr. HUM, the master of them all, is a creature we have created."

"Hear! Hear!" everybody shouted again. Everybody also clapped vigorously.

The man held up his hand to indicate that he had not finished.

"If anybody has gone mad," he said somberly, "it is the man who programs Mr. HUM."

He sat down, drawing his knees up to his chin and leaning on them.

The room was totally silent. The scientists stared at each other. Gradually they began to murmur, "Who? "Who? Who?" The word sounded and resounded all over the room.

Mr. Humwhistel slowly rose to his feet.

"I'm quite sure that I know who it is," he said very quietly. "I don't know, however, whether I'll be able to stop him. He is power mad. And he has the control."

Miss Pickerell felt so furious she could no longer contain herself.

"I don't care if he controls the universe," she called out. "I cannot approve of him."

The scientists stood up and shouted, "Bravo!"

"May I come up and say something?" Miss Pickerell asked Ms. Whitechurch. "I don't remember the speech I prepared. But I must give my point of view."

"Please," Ms. Whitechurch said.

Miss Pickerell walked to the head of the table. She turned around to face the scientists.

"I don't understand all I should about computers," she began. "I depend upon Mr. Humwhistel and upon Euphus, my middle nephew, for that."

The scientists nodded their approval.

"I understand better," Miss Pickerell went on, "about kindness and about love between animals and people. Why, my friend, Mr. Kettelson, would die if anything happened to my cow. And Nancy Pickett, my oldest niece Rosemary's best friend, would get sick if they took her lamb away from her. She'd never forget the pain, even if she lived to be a hundred. She'd think of it from time to time and . . ."

She stopped for a moment to push down the sobs that were beginning to get into her voice. Then she described the things that had been happening in Square Toe County.

"And," she said after she had repeated Mr. Gilhuly's account of Square Toe City and added precisely what she thought of the City of Progress, "I am of the opinion that life without the freedom to live peacefully with the people and the animals and the flowers and even the colors that you love is not life at all. I want to say too that I am going to stick to my opinion."

Miss Pickerell interrupted the applause that followed.

"That isn't everything," she said miserably. "The computer has just announced that all animals over eight years old must be destroyed. That means my cow."

"Never!" Mr. Humwhistel and the deputy administrator both shouted.

"And by tomorrow," Miss Pickerell added hurriedly, "he may say that I'm to be destroyed, too. I'm more than eight years old. Even if you count in animal years the way the veterinarians tell you to, I think I'm more than eight years old."

The scientists roared their protest. Ms. Whitechurch had a hard time getting them to quiet down.

"Order! Order!" she called. "I will now entertain suggestions from the floor."

The man in the turtleneck sweater got up.

"I cannot say with certainty at this point," he stated, "whether the computers have taken over from man or not. One thing is clear, however. They intend to banish life from this planet. We are aware of this. That is why we are meeting here today. Our chairlady, Ms. Whitechurch, was wise enough to realize the urgency when she insisted upon calling us together."

Ms. Whitechurch smiled modestly.

The tall young man raised his hand. Ms. Whitechurch recognized him. He unwound his knees and stood up.

"Who cares," he asked hoarsely, "whether it is a mad computer who has taken over from man or a man who has gone mad who is feeding the computer? The essential point is that we have to stop this. We have to stop this monstrous destruction at once!"

"Short-circuit the computer!" the scientists shouted with one voice. "Short-circuit the computer! Short-circuit it *now!*"

Mr. Humwhistel raised his hand. Ms. Whitechurch called on him to speak.

"I happen to think," he said as he sucked on his pipe furiously, "that the fault is with the person who is feeding directions into the computer and I intend to follow this up. But I agree with my colleagues that we must act immediately to short-circuit the computer. Unfortunately . . ."

He paused. The room was so quiet it seemed to Miss Pickerell that no one was even breathing.

"Unfortunately," Mr. Humwhistel resumed, putting his pipe in his pocket, "I am afraid we may be too late."

He paused again. The silence was almost unbearable. Miss Pickerell was afraid she was going to scream.

"From what I have been able to learn," Mr. Humwhistel continued, "a very exact plan has been set up. If the computer is proceeding on its prescribed schedule, we are at this very moment Mr. HUM's prisoners. And the world we live in may soon come crashing down around . . ."

A peal like thunder drowned out the end of his sentence. Miss Pickerell sank into the chair next to the desk and closed her eyes.

"Forevermore!" she breathed. "Forevermore!"

CHAPTER THIRTEEN

WHAT EUPHUS DID

The roar stopped as suddenly as it had begun. A tremendous shaking took its place. Miss Pickerell clutched the edges of her seat to keep from falling out of it. Ms. Whitechurch, standing behind Miss Pickerell, clung to the back of the chair. Deputy Administrator Blakely, who had moved up to them, supported Ms. Whitechurch by her elbow. Mr. Humwhistel took his pipe out of his pocket and hunted for matches.

Nobody said a word when the shaking subsided. Miss Pickerell searched frantically in her mind for some explanation. She couldn't find any. And Mr. Humwhistel and the deputy administrator were no help either. They just stood there, looking baffled. Ms. Whitechurch, for once, seemed too flabbergasted to act. Miss Pickerell was just about to ask her to call the meeting to order again when she heard Pumpkins' meow at the door.

"That's ridiculous," she told herself, while she clutched her heart which had begun to pound at something like a mile a minute. "I really must stop imagining things."

But it *was* Pumpkins' meow, deep and insistently loud. There was no mistaking it.

And then Miss Pickerell heard the gentle mooing of a cow and the soft bleat of a lamb and the yelping of a puppy and voices, human voices, that she recognized only too well as the chattering of her seven nieces and nephews. Nobody else seemed to be hearing them. The scientists were simply staring at each other.

"We're saved!" one of them finally murmured and then another and then another until the murmur became a roar.

The noise at the door was even louder. Miss Pickerell decided that the scientists had all gone stone deaf, perhaps with shock. She marched briskly to the door and opened it.

Mr. Kettelson was right there in front of her. He was beaming almost as broadly as

Mr. Rugby, who stood beside him. Her cow walked quietly between them. Miss Pickerell bent down immediately to hug the cow. She hugged Rosemary, too, and Pumpkins, who was in Rosemary's arms, and Nancy, who had her lamb at her side and a small brown dog in her arms and who was trying to tell her that she found the dog when they were collecting animals and that he didn't seem to belong to anybody and that she loved him and was keeping him and . . .

Mr. Rugby's shouting was making it impossible for her to listen to Nancy.

"Euphus did it!" he was screaming triumphantly. "Euphus fixed the computer!"

Dwight and Dr. Haggerty and Mr. Gilhuly and Mr. Kettelson and Homer and Harry, her twin nephews, and the rest of her nieces and nephews joined him in an ear-splitting chorus.

"Euphus!" Deputy Administrator Blakely bellowed over their voices. "Is this true?"

"Euphus!" Miss Pickerell called. "Please come here immediately!"

Euphus moved up from the rear. Rosemary gave him a little push when he passed her to make him walk faster.

"Sure," he said, when he stood facing Miss Pickerell. "Sure, I did it. Right after you left, Aunt Lavinia."

"You couldn't have," the deputy administrator said, towering sternly above him.

"Of course, I could," Euphus replied. "It was easy."

"Easy . . ." Mr. Humwhistel murmured.

"Very," Euphus said. "I just changed the cards."

"Which cards?" Miss Pickerell asked.

"The computer cards, of course," Euphus said. "What other cards are there?"

"No!" Mr. Humwhistel muttered incredulously, his hand instantly popping his pipe into his mouth.

"Yes," Euphus said. "I figured that the only way to stop the computer on its present course was to feed it some cards that would reprogram it with new instructions."

"Very reasonable," Miss Pickerell commented.

Ms. Whitechurch nodded her head in agreement. "And Euphus probably caused the computer breakdown that landed you in the conference room instead of on Mars!"

The scientist in the turtleneck sweater remarked that he wasn't sure about that. The very tall scientist argued that he was very sure.

"And the roar and the shaking came when all the Square Toe County computers changed course," he said. "I understand perfectly."

"I guess I do, too," the first scientist said a little grudgingly.

"So do I! So do I!" all the other scientists chimed in.

Miss Pickerell smiled faintly. She could hardly believe that this . . . this miracle had really happened, that they were actually safe now from all the horror, the senseless cruelty. She tried to kiss Euphus.

"Oh, it was nothing," Euphus said,

squirming away and looking very red and embarrassed. "I just went to see my science teacher when I got the idea about the computer. He had some computer cards and he helped me make them out. He also told me where to go to make the change."

"Where?" Ms. Whitechurch, Mr. Humwhistel, and Mr. Blakely asked at once.

"Oh, in an old warehouse, not far from the school, where they keep the local computer," Euphus told them. "My teacher knows the people in charge. They gave him permission once to take some advanced science classes through the place so they could see how it all worked. I'm going next year. My teacher says I'm very advanced in science."

Miss Pickerell had no doubts about that.

"But where were the people in charge when you and your teacher went there?" she asked, not really believing her ears. "Didn't they stop you? Didn't they . . . ?"

"Oh," Euphus explained, "they didn't know we were going to do it. They thought my teacher was just going to show things to me. They weren't even in the room when we changed the cards."

"I see," Miss Pickerell said vaguely.

A thousand thoughts were going through her head. One of them was about the people in the warehouse. She wondered if one of them was the mad scientist responsible for Mr. H.U.M. She wondered when he would be caught and punished. She was sure that Mr. Humwhistel would see to it. The question that really bothered her though was whether Euphus had broken the law. She was turning it over and over in her mind when Euphus thrust her unfinished head scarf into her hands.

"I nearly forgot," he said. "One of the ladies from the Why Not Knit It Department came up to the house just before we left. She said to give it to you. She said that knitting has a calming effect on people."

Miss Pickerell automatically began to wind the wool around her left forefinger. The needles clicked while she carefully listened to the scientists questioning Euphus. She breathed an enormous sigh of relief when she gathered from the tone of their voices that Euphus had not really done anything wrong. She stuffed the scarf into her knitting bag and said that she thought it was time for them all to go home.

Mr. Rugby immediately detached the trailer from his truck. Mr. Kettelson attached it to Miss Pickerell's automobile and gently led the cow and Pumpkins inside. He settled himself comfortably next to them. Deputy Administrator Blakely escorted Miss Pickerell and Ms. Whitechurch into the front of the automobile. He, Mr. Humwhistel, and Euphus sat in the back. Rosemary, Dwight, and Nancy went with Mr. Rugby. Mr. Gilhuly piled all the rest of the children and animals into his Rural Free Delivery truck.

Mr. Blakely offered Miss Pickerell his three maps as soon as he closed the door of the automobile.

"Thank you, Deputy Administrator," Miss Pickerell said. "I think I can find my way without them. I was watching the route very carefully when we came."

She drove cautiously back through the City of Progress. She was glad to see that some things had already changed for the better. The traffic lights were working. And the men at the excavation site were no longer throwing the dirt back in. Some people were also cleaning the wreckage out of the river under the little, humpbacked bridge. Miss Pickerell felt considerably relieved.

The mare and her foal and the cow and her calf were still in the meadow when she passed. She waved happily to them. She also waved to the birds sipping water at the next river. She sneaked a glance into her rearview mirror. Mr. Humwhistel and Mr. Blakely were plying Euphus with questions.

"I think I'll just drive through Square Toe City," she whispered to herself. "They're so busy talking they won't know the difference."

Miss Pickerell nearly cried when she saw the dismal streets with their sad gardens and their bleak, dark houses. But she felt better as she drove along. In front of a number of houses, men were standing on ladders with paint brushes in their hands. One man had already finished painting his window frames. Miss Pickerell was happy to observe that they were bright pink. And a little further on, people were reseeding their gardens.

By the time she passed Lemon Lane and approached the turn that led into her private road all she could think of was how hungry she was. In her mind's eye she could even see the thick slices of bread and butter she would have with her tea. She invited Ms. Whitechurch, Mr. Kettelson, Mr. Humwhistel, and Mr. Blakely to join her. Mr. Kettelson accepted. The others declined politely. They had arranged for Euphus to show them the exact location of the warehouse. Miss Pickerell thought it was very correct of them to do this so promptly.

"Not too much bread and butter, Miss Pickerell," Deputy Administrator Blakely warned when he was helping her out of the car. "Mr. Rugby is giving a party this evening in your honor. You wouldn't want to disappoint him by not eating his eclipse specials."

Miss Pickerell shuddered slightly at the idea of a party in her honor. But she wouldn't hurt Mr. Rugby's feelings for anything.

"I can always eat an eclipse special," she said as she lifted Pumpkins from the trailer, asked Mr. Kettelson to lead the cow into the pasture, and walked happily into her kitchen.

CHAPTER FOURTEEN

SQUARE TOE FARM
IS ON THE MAP AGAIN

Everybody came to Miss Pickerell's party. The Governor greeted Miss Pickerell at the door of the diner when she arrived.

"Square Toe Farm is on the map again," he said the instant he saw her. "I told you I would attend to it."

Miss Pickerell nodded.

"Have some peppermints," the Governor offered, taking a bagful out of his pocket. "I brought them especially for you. I know how you love peppermint."

Miss Pickerell took only two.

"I'm not very hungry, thank you, Governor," she said.

"You will be," Mr. Rugby, listening nearby, promised. He led her through the door to a long table in the center of the restaurant and placed a moonburger in front of her. Miss Pickerell ate it immediately. Mr. Rugby raced to get another.

The Governor came and sat down on the right of Miss Pickerell. Mr. Rugby put Mr. Humwhistel, Mr. Blakely, and the editor of the *Square Toe Gazette* alongside the Governor. Euphus, Ms. Whitechurch, and the lady reporter from the *Gazette* were on Miss Pickerell's left. The lady reporter had on a long dress and a floppy hat with yellow, polka-dot ribbons. She was writing down every word in a blue spiral notebook.

The crowd kept pouring in. Miss Pickerell saw her brother and his wife and the rest of her seven nieces and nephews and Dr. Haggerty and Mr. Gilhuly and Nancy and Mr. and Mrs. Pickett and Mr. Esticott, the baggage master, who had been away visiting his daughter in Plentibush City, and Mr. Squeers, who had a camera slung over each shoulder, and even the three ladies from the Why Not Knit It Department. Mr. Kettelson was the last to arrive. He came with the cow. He sat in the back so that he could keep an eye on her through the rear window.

There were a lot of other people Miss Pickerell did not know. She guessed they were scientists. And there were television men putting cables down all over the restaurant and photographers popping up every few minutes at Miss Pickerell's table to take a picture. Miss Pickerell kept smiling politely.

The Governor got up as soon as Mr. Rugby closed the door.

"I know," he said as he smoothed his moustache, "that you expect me to say something. Let me start by announcing that Miss Pickerell has done it again. Yes, Miss Pickerell has enabled me to put Square Toe Farm back on the map."

He bowed to Miss Pickerell. Miss Pickerell bowed back. The cameras clicked.

"But, more important," he went on, "she has saved us in Square Toe County from a terrible disaster. She has saved us from a machine-controlled society that would have robbed us all of our freedom."

He paused for a drink of water. Mr. Rugby quickly refilled his glass.

"Now, machines have their place," the Governor continued. "Miss Pickerell knows that. She knows that I believe in progress. As Governor of this State, I have the responsibility of working for progress."

He cleared his throat.

"But," he said almost immediately while he banged hard on the table, "but machines *must* be kept in their place. And Miss Pickerell has shown us *that*!"

"Miss Pickerell! Miss Pickerell!"

The words burst from every throat in the room. Thunderous applause accompanied the shouts.

The Governor helped Miss Pickerell out of her chair. Mr. Rugby rushed over with a bouquet of roses that he placed on the table in front of her. There's no mistaking those delicate pink petals, Miss Pickerell thought, Mr. Rugby has grown these himself.

"Thank you, Mr. Rugby," she said.

"Speech! Speech!" everybody called.

Miss Pickerell took a breath.

"I'm not really the one who should be making the speech," she said. "It's my middle nephew, Euphus, who thought up a way to stop the local computer, and the scientists are now going to do what is needed with the other computers, too. All I know is that I

didn't trust the computer when it began to do things against animals. It's my opinion that you can never trust anyone who doesn't like animals. You never know what such a person—or machine—is going to do next. And this computer didn't like animals *or* people. It only liked machines. I *had* to stop it."

Mr. Rugby wiped his doughy hands on his white apron and applauded. So did everyone else. It was during the applause that Miss Pickerell noticed an angry man being led away by Mr. Humwhistel and Deputy Administrator Blakely. They had tracked down the mad scientist. Miss Pickerell sighed with relief. She was so glad he was no one she knew.

"Anyway," Miss Pickerell went on as the crowd grew quiet, "it all started when I was trying to think of a name for my cow. I have finally found one that I think she will like. I am naming her after two people. The first is a little girl who adopts every stray animal that comes her way. The second is the fine young woman who called the meeting to halt the activities of the terrible Mr. HUM. I am naming my cow Nancy, short for Nancy Pickett, and Agatha, short for Ms. Agatha Whitechurch. Nancy Agatha is a good name for a good animal. I thank you."

The applause that followed was almost as loud as the roar that had filled the meeting room when the computers shifted course. But nobody was standing still this time. Ms. Whitechurch leaned over to say that she was proud to have Miss Pickerell's cow named after her. Nancy hugged Rosemary and jumped up and down with joy. And all through the room the photographers were shouting, "Where's the cow? Where's the cow?" Mr. Squeers was the first to get to her. He snapped picture after picture and raced back to tell Miss Pickerell that his photographs would definitely turn out better than any of the others.

Miss Pickerell smiled happily. She was thinking that she would certainly have a lot of pictures to choose from. She would enlarge and put a silver frame around the best one. She knew exactly where to hang it, right over the horsehair sofa where she liked to lie down with Pumpkins at her feet for a little rest.

Then a thought occurred to her, and she leaned over toward Euphus.

"Euphus, I've been meaning to ask you, how did you ever find us? Mr. HUM's headquarters were top secret."

"I used a tracking device," whispered Euphus.

"You must never do that again," Miss Pickerell said in a horrified voice.

"I won't," Euphus promised, and jumped up to lead a cheer for his favorite aunt.

Miss Pickerell shook her head. It was not likely that she'd get much rest, certainly not with a nephew like Euphus. Perhaps, she decided, it would be best to order two enlargements framed. She would hang the second one on the long middle wall of her neat, comfortable farmhouse kitchen.

ABOUT THE AUTHORS

Ellen MacGregor created the character of Miss Pickerell in the early 1950's. With a little help from Miss MacGregor, Lavinia Pickerell had four remarkable adventures: *Miss Pickerell Goes to Mars, Miss Pickerell and the Geiger Counter, Miss Pickerell Goes Undersea*, and *Miss Pickerell Goes to the Arctic*. Then, in 1954, Ellen MacGregor died, leaving behind boxes filled with notes for future Miss Pickerell plots. While young fans wrote, begging for more Miss Pickerell books, McGraw-Hill searched and searched for a writer who could capture Miss P's special character and take her on new and exciting adventures. Then Miss P. found Dora Pantell.

Dora Pantell is an assistant director for the New York City Board of Education where she supervises programs in reading and in English as a second language. She has taught adults and children of all ages for the Board of Education, has prepared curriculum materials for teachers and students, and has appeared on weekly television programs which she wrote and produced. She has also written radio documentaries, materials on illiteracy for the federal government's anti-poverty program, films, magazine stories, and books. Her most recent book is *If Not Now, When: The Many Meanings of Black Power* (Delacorte Press). Ms. Pantell shares her Manhattan apartment with her three cats, Haiku, Figaro, and Eliza Doolittle.

ABOUT THE ARTIST

Charles Geer has been illustrating for as long as he can remember and has more books to his credit than he can count. He and his wife Mary, their four grown children, and one cat live in the woods near Flemington, New Jersey in a log cabin Charles built himself. When he is not bent over the drawing board or the typewriter— Mr. Geer has written as well as illustrated two middle-group books—he takes long back-pack hikes, camps out in wilderness, and loves to sail.

Library of Congress Cataloging in Publication Data

MacGregor, Ellen.
  Miss Pickerell meets Mr. H.U.M.

  SUMMARY: Miss Pickerell was trying to think of a
name for her cow when the telephone rang and plunged
her into a horrifying chain of events.
  [1. Computers—Fiction] I. Pantell, Dora F.,
joint author. II. Geer, Charles, illus. III. Title.
PZ7.M1698Mot   [Fic]   74-2126
ISBN 0-07-044577-X
ISBN 0-07-044578-8 (lib. bdg.)

160